The Mystery of

Charles Dickens

A Tale of

Mesmerism and Murder

By

John Paulits

Copyright

Paperback ISBN 9781780921778
ePub ISBN 9781780921785
PDF ISBN 9781780921792

Published in the UK by MX Publishing
335 Princess Park Manor, Royal Drive,
London, N11 3GX
www.mxpublishing.com
Cover design by www.staunch.com

To Kirk and Shirley

Contents

PROLOGUE

Charles Dickens had been unwell for some time. Neuralgia on the left side of his face punished him with periods of utter misery. Kidney spasms, a nemesis since childhood, prostrated him on occasion. His left foot, often swollen and painful, made his daily twelve-mile walks a thing of the past. His left hand had begun to disobey his commands, and the sight in his left eye caused him concern. His public readings had caused a deterioration in his health impossible to counter, yet he bore up and continued working on *The Mystery of Edwin Drood*. He approached this book differently from his other books, however. For one thing, it would have only twelve monthly numbers rather than his usual twenty. In his contract for the book, he insisted on a clause detailing what monies would be returned to his publishers, Chapman and Hall, in the event he could not finish the book. He knew completing *Drood* involved a race against his own mortality.

June 6, 1870, a Monday. Dickens rises about seven, maintaining the rigid schedule he needs to give shape and meaning to his day. His work routine must run like clockwork or he cannot even begin his day's writing. It is a lovely morning in Rochester, twenty-five miles southeast of London, as Dickens takes a morning tour of his Gad's Hill home and grounds to assure himself everything is in its place. He breakfasts, then walks through the garden to the tunnel he has had constructed under the Rochester High Road. The tunnel leads to a piece of property he owns, where a Swiss chalet stands. His family calls his retreat "The Wilderness."

The chalet is a small, two-story structure with an outside stairway given to him in 1864 as a Christmas gift (in fifty-eight boxes!) by Charles Fechter, a French-born actor and regular Sunday visitor to Gad's Hill, and it is on the chalet's second floor that Dickens writes in fair weather. Before settling in, though, he looks over his desk to be certain everything is in its place—the goose quill pens and his blue ink; sheets of blue-gray paper 8 ¾ inches by 7 ¼ inches; the bronze statue of two toads dueling; a small china monkey; a paper knife; a gilt leaf with a rabbit on it. These are the things his eye rests familiarly upon in moments of contemplation. His crystal carafe of water sits at his elbow. He sets to work.

Kate, his married daughter, is returning to London and, knowing her father's distaste for farewells, originally plans to leave without seeing him. Such a cold good-bye does not feel right on this day, however. The night before, she had sat up late with her father and feels uneasy at a remark he made. In their conversation he said he hoped he would be able to finish his new book. Hoped. So, she makes her way through the garden tunnel to the chalet and climbs the staircase. Instead of his usual brief farewell, her father rises and embraces her. She leaves and Dickens returns to *Edwin Drood.*

Dickens follows his usual work schedule the next day, Tuesday. He writes until one then lunches in the main house. Instead of the accustomed three-hour-long walk he previously took in better days to fill up the time between his writing and dinner, he rides in a carriage to nearby Cobham Wood with his sister-in-law, Georgina Hogarth, and they take a much briefer walk.

The next day, the final day on which Dickens would

2

ever write a word, he deviates from his schedule. He writes until one, but after lunch smokes a cigar in his study, no doubt contemplating where to take the plot of his story. Then he goes back to the chalet and writes through the afternoon until nearly five. He throws down his quill just after Datchery, a mysterious character newly introduced to the tale, learns something which pleases him to excess. Datchery marks a strange chalk tally on his door, orders a meal, and "falls to with an appetite."

Dickens returns to the house, and though he feels ill, he writes two letters. In one letter he promises to see his correspondent, a Charles Kent, in London the next day at three—no doubt after a morning's work. He writes, though, "If I can't be—why, then I shan't be."

Only he and his sister-in-law, Georgina, dine at Gad's Hill that evening. When they come to the table, Georgina sees from his expression something is wrong. She asks whether he is ill. He says he is and has been for the past hour. He dismisses her suggestion of sending for Doctor Steele, the local doctor, saying he plans on traveling to London after dinner.

Then it happens.

Georgina watches him struggle with something sweeping over him. He speaks incoherently and indistinctly. She rises from her chair and goes to help him, saying he should lie down, but he is struggling, wavering, and he is too heavy for her.

"Yes," he says. "On the ground." He collapses.

3

Doctors are summoned, one local, Doctor Steele; one a friend, Dr. Frank Beard, who arrives from London; and one a noted physician also from London, Dr. Russell Reynolds, who arrives the next day. The prognosis of each is the same. He cannot live. Dickens lingers some twenty-four hours lying on a sofa brought into the dining room where he collapsed, his loud, heavy breathing no doubt chilling those who gather at his side hoping to see his eyes open, hoping to detect some movement, anything to indicate his return to them.

At six o'clock in the evening on the day after his collapse, Dickens' breathing quiets. As the gathered mourners watch, a tear wells up in Dickens' right eye and rolls gently down his cheek. He heaves a deep sigh and breathes no more.

And so history proclaims that on Thursday, June 9, 1870, England's greatest novelist died of a cerebral hemorrhage. History is wrong. June 9, 1870 is the day on which Emile de la Rue murdered Charles Dickens.

How can I claim such a thing?

The following narrative is based primarily on two pieces of evidence I uncovered writing my own biography of Dickens. John Forster, Dickens' best friend and first biographer, provided me with the initial inkling of this story when I went through some boxes of Forster's original papers which, clearly, no one had inspected with any great care. The short manuscript I found told a story dictated to him by Dickens—a story which never made it into Forster's biography. Perhaps Forster feared that including such a fantastic tale would damage his credibility. More likely, after Dickens' death he had no way to corroborate the

4

story's claims. At any rate, he kept it secret. The manuscript told the story of the ghost which haunted both Augusta de la Rue and Charles Dickens. I had no way to confirm the story either, so taking my cue from Forster, I left it out of my biography. But the shocking news in Forster's notes ate at me—became a ghost to me also you might say. I began digging.

After a near twenty-month investigation, I managed to find a descendant of the de la Rues living in Italy—Genoa to be precise—a very old woman—a cousin, once removed, of a great-granddaughter. To make a long story short, she let me inspect her attic, home to the family records.

Beneath some moldering nineteenth century business documents, I found a diary kept by Emile de la Rue in flawless English, detailing his relationship with Charles Dickens.

De la Rue began the diary in 1844 on the day he first met Dickens in Italy and put it aside when Dickens left Italy in the late spring of 1845. The diary started up again in 1869 when de la Rue met Dickens in London at the Athenaeum Club and continued until Dickens' death.

What Emile de la Rue wrote seemed impossible, but I knew he told the truth since not only did the diary confirm the information in Forster's manuscript, it took the story to lengths unknown to Forster.

Everything you are going to read is based on de la Rue's diary, Forster's suppressed notes, or my own research. It is quite a tale.

Chapter One

On Tuesday, July 20, 1869, John Forster sat at his desk. He was not a tall man though his bulk and round, jowly face gave him the illusion of being quite large. Opinionated, pugnacious, and sure of himself, Forster became the self-appointed, generally acknowledged keeper of the Dickens literary flame. He looked over his mail and saw an envelope with Charles Dickens' handwriting. He opened it first. In part Dickens had written:

> *What should you think of the idea of a story beginning in this way? Two people, boy and girl, or very young, going apart from one another, pledged to be married after many years—at the end of the book. The interest to arise out of the tracing of their separate ways, and the impossibility of telling what will be done with that impending fate.*

The note went on to say that Dickens expected to be in town Thursday and Friday. Thursday was "make up" day at the offices of *All The Year Round*, a weekly magazine Dickens edited, and Dickens always took the lead in putting the magazine together. Nothing went into the magazine without his specific approval and frequently his editorial re-writing. The note invited Forster to meet him at the Athenaeum for dinner on Thursday at six.

Forster reread the note. He thought Dickens' intention to write another novel an encouraging sign. It had been some four years since the previous novel, a relatively unsuccessful one by Dickens' standards. *Our Mutual Friend* had begun its nineteen-month run selling upwards of 35,000 monthly numbers but ended selling no more than 19,000. Though Forster reminded Dickens that 19,000 was still four times as many as Thackeray had ever sold for any book he had ever written, Dickens felt depressed. He subsequently launched himself on a killing regimen of public readings in America and England until his doctors forced him to stop, and Forster welcomed anything that would get Dickens to sit still and perhaps tend to his health.

The Athenaeum, located at 107 Pall Mall SW in London and founded in 1824, described itself as an "association of individuals known for their scientific and literary attainments, artists of eminence in any class of the fine arts and noblemen and gentlemen distinguished as liberal patrons of science, literature or the arts." The club took itself very seriously, and Dickens loved being acknowledged as one of its most noted members.

Forster stood chatting with someone at the bottom of the twenty-three steps of the grand staircase when Dickens arrived as always in a bustle, his hat perched cockily on his head. It seemed he would let nothing—neither health nor high water—slow him down.

"John, John, how are you?" He shook Forster's hand energetically.

"Fine, Charles. You look well."

"I feel well. The foot is behaving itself, thank

Heaven. I think I'll walk tonight after we eat. Follow me."

Dickens led the way up the stairs and through the hall to the coffee room. The gas-fed chandelier in the middle of the room was as yet unlit. He led Forster across the room to an empty table near a window overlooking Pall Mall, nodding at people as he went. *How he loves to be seen,* Forster thought.

When they were seated, Forster grinned and said, "You've left your yellow waistcoat back at Gad's Hill, I hope."

"Don't mock me, John, or I'll walk there right now and get it."

Forster laughed. "I believe you would."

"Red suits me, though, don't you think?" Dickens patted himself on the chest.

They ordered and Dickens immediately asked, "What do you think of my idea, John?"

Forster had never been shy about giving Dickens his opinion of his ideas. Whether Dickens heeded Forster's advice was another matter.

"I don't see the uniqueness of it, to be honest. It echoes the Wilfer girl and Rokesmith in *Friend.*"

"No, no, no, John. You're wrong. I can *make* it unique. I haven't written a tale in, what, four years? I have ideas. Good ideas."

Dickens changed the subject to his day at his Wellington Street North office. Forster knew Dickens did not want an argument from him. He wanted to be right. So Forster listened with interest to the report of Dickens' day, interjecting questions and comments.

Suddenly, Dickens' face went white. A stab of fear shot through Forster. Was Dickens having an attack? Dickens stared past Forster, over his shoulder. Forster turned. Two men in their sixties had newly entered the coffee room. Forster turned back to his companion.

"Do you know them?"

"One of them," Dickens answered. "The clean-shaven one."

Forster turned again. The man Dickens indicated had noticed him and stopped while his companion, unaware, continued on.

"He's coming over, Charles," Forster whispered.

The clean-shaven man dressed immaculately. No red waistcoat for him, however. He had chosen a deep and serious gray one to compliment his dark blue suit. For some reason he had not checked his stick and made of show of it as he approached Dickens' table. Dickens rose and Forster followed suit. The man stood taller than Dickens—most men did—and with a slight backward movement of his head seemed to stare down his nose at Dickens. His wavy white hair seemed an appropriate crown for him.

"Charles," the man said.

Dickens nodded curtly. "Emile."

"It has been a long time." The man spoke with a slight French accent.

"Yes, it has."

"I presume you've heard about Augusta?"

"I heard she passed away a few years ago."

Emile glanced down. "Yes."

"It must have been a great relief to you," Dickens

9

said.

Forster looked at him. What the devil could Dickens mean by that he wondered?

Emile cocked his head. "I'm sorry?"

"Her passing must have been a relief from her sufferings. And yours."

"Oh, I see. Yes, she had been ill for some time. The old malady, you know. There was no cure."

At those words Dickens stared coldly at the man. The waiter arrived with his and Forster's dinners.

"I see you are about to dine. I don't wish to hold you back."

"Nor I you," Dickens replied. Emile had accompanied each of his sentences with a small smile. Dickens had yet to smile.

"Good evening, then." Emile turned away and moved off to the other side of the room to rejoin his friend. Forster noticed Dickens and the man had foregone handshakes.

"What in the world was that about?" Forster asked when he and Dickens resumed their seats. "*Who* in the world is that man?"

"He," said Dickens with what seemed a misplaced intensity to Forster, "is Emile de la Rue. Kate and I met him and his wife, Augusta, twenty-five years ago in Genoa, the year we stayed in Italy."

"Don't I remember your writing me you did some of your hocus-pocus on the wife for some reason?"

Dickens eyes pierced Forster's like white-hot pokers.

"Let's eat, John."

Forster knew Dickens would speak no more of de la

Rue that night.

On Wednesday of the next week, Forster received another note from Dickens. It read in part:

> ...laid aside the fancy I told you of, and have a very curious and new idea for my new story. Not a communicable idea (or the interest of the book would be gone), but a very strong one, though difficult to work.

The rest of the note vacillated between Dickens' certainty of the merits of the story and the difficulties he would encounter in bringing it to life. In a postscript Dickens asked Forster whether he would be able to come to Gad's Hill for the weekend. He had something he wanted to discuss with him.

Forster immediately accepted Dickens' invitation and wrote him so next day. Mulling over Dickens' behavior at the Athenaeum and the conflicting tone of his latest note, Forster asked around the Athenaeum about the strange man, Emile de la Rue. Satisfied he had found out all he could, Forster took the train out of London to Rochester late Friday afternoon.

Dickens welcomed him to Gad's Hill, and after dinner they sat with the Dickens women—daughters Kate, who had come down from London, and Mamie, and sister-in-law Georgina. The conversation after dinner centered around Dickens' eldest son Charley and what a fine job he did helping out on *All The Year Round* since William Wills, the day-to-day editor of the magazine, took a leave to recuperate from a concussion received in a fall from a horse. The conversation then turned to Dickens' youngest son, Henry, affectionately called "little Plorn" by the family. He had emigrated to Australia the previous September to join his brother Alfred. The family discussed his chances of succeeding as well as how much they missed him. Dickens made no mention of either de la Rue or his new story.

The next day, however, at the conclusion of lunch, Dickens said, "John, come with me to the chalet. I want to have a talk with you."

Something about the change in Dickens' tone sent a tremor through Forster.

"Certainly, Charles," and he followed Dickens out into the garden and the riot of blooming geraniums—Dickens favorite flower and standard buttonhole when he stood upon a stage to read—through the tunnel and into the chalet.

Chapter Two

Dickens pointed to one of the two red sofas facing each other on the first floor of the chalet. Forster sat and watched Dickens circle the room, opening windows. Along with the sofas the first floor was furnished with two chairs, a bookcase, two wall mirrors and a long table against the wall holding some potted geraniums. A large, purple, oval rug covered most of the floor.

Dickens approached Forster carrying a cigar box.

"Cigar, John? I'd offer you a drink. You may need one soon, but it's rather early in the day."

"Cigar is fine." Forster never turned down one of Dickens' Havanas, his standard cigar since his return from Italy twenty-five years before.

Dickens replaced the box in the bookcase and returned to sit across from Forster. Both men took a few moments to attend to the lighting of their cigars. A long, low table sat between the two sofas, and on it were two glass ashtrays and a lone pot of geraniums.

"Business first, John," Dickens began. "As I wrote you, I've changed my mind about the topic of my new story." He pulled strongly on his cigar, leaned his head back, and blew the smoke straight up. "I'm planning only twelve monthly parts..."

"Twelve! Why not the usual twenty?"

"John, let's be truthful. You know I haven't been well, and I want very much to complete this story. The day

13

we dined was the last healthy day I've had. This past weekend I could barely move because of my accursed foot. I've half a mind to lop it off and be content with hobbling about pain-free. Sometimes when I look at signs on the street, I can only make out the right-hand side. The blood I lose...but you know all of this. Let's not go over it again." Forster knew of Dickens severe case of piles. "And my will is made."

Dickens had previously told Forster about his will, which he'd completed two months earlier.

"If I can't finish this book, John, I want it in the contract with Chapman and Hall that you will arbitrate the amount of money to be returned to them. They're giving me seventy-five hundred pounds."

"Charles, what are you saying? Of course you'll complete the book."

Dickens nodded absent-mindedly. "My new idea came to me when I saw that villain de la Rue."

"I thought as much. I've asked about him around the club."

"And?"

"Seems he's newly in London and has taken up with Lord Allsgood. They met in Europe and de la Rue is here at his invitation. Allsgood has leased him one of his homes, The Kensington House. I think he means to stay in England."

"The man is a...a...scoundrel, John!" Brought up on and a life-long fan of the melodramatic theatre of his day, Dickens, in his momentary passion, could think of no term so damning as the one he used. "I know him, John. I know what he is and I know what he's done, and I am going to reveal it to everyone by means of my book. I will expose his crime for all of England, for all the *world*, to see."

"Charles, be calm." Forster rose, touched Dickens on the shoulder, paced a moment behind the sofa, and sat again. "You haven't seen the man in years. You're overwrought. What could he possibly...?"

"What could he possibly? I've asked you here today because I want to tell you a story I've never shared with a soul, not even Ellen." Ellen was Ellen Ternan, a young actress with whom Dickens had been close for many years since he had separated from his wife. "I will tell you what he did and then see whether you can tell me he should not be exposed."

With his right hand Forster gestured for Dickens to begin.

"It began twenty-five years ago. Our first prolonged trip to the continent..."

Charles Dickens, thirty-two years old in 1844, decided to leave England. It had been a trying year. He and his wife Catherine produced babies—expensive babies—at an alarming rate. His father continually contracted debts Dickens always paid off for him. He had brothers and sisters dependent on him. Money cascaded from him like a waterfall. *A Christmas Carol*, although a popular book, had been expensive to produce—Dickens insisted on color illustrations—and, although selling well this past Christmas, did not make the profit Dickens anticipated. His latest book, *The Adventures of Martin Chuzzlewit,* had been less than a success, and when it did not justify the advance given him by Chapman and Hall, Edward Hall inadvisably reminded Dickens of a penalty clause in their contract covering such an eventuality. Dickens became livid, insulted, and vengeful. In debt to Chapman and Hall for his unmet advance on *Chuzzlewit*, he worked out an agreement with Bradbury and Evans to be his new publishers. He took a large advance from them; paid off Chapman and Hall; rented out his Devonshire Terrace home to a widow; bought an immense old stage coach for forty-five pounds; and packed the family off to Italy, which had a far more reasonable cost of living than England. With a second Christmas book he planned to write, along with a travel book on his experiences in Italy, Dickens intended to come back home a solvent man.

The enormous coach could fit twelve, the size of his traveling band, and came complete with some extraordinary contrivances—a multitude of storage compartments and a reading lamp chief among them. It required the services of four horses and, to control them, a postilion, who wore a pair of immense, spurred jack-boots and who had a propensity to cry, "En route—Hi!" whenever the carriage began to roll. The travelers consisted of Dickens, his wife Catherine, his seventeen-year-old sister-in-law Georgina, Catherine's maid Anne Brown, two other domestic servants, and the five children; Charley, Mary, Kate, Walter and baby Frank, known in the family as Chickenstalker. Charley, the eldest, was seven. The family dog Timber Doodle also went along.

The twelfth member of the group was Louis Roche, a portly man and native of Avignon, who had the title "courier." His responsibilities encompassed writing ahead to secure rooms for the Dickens entourage, negotiating their bills and, in general, smoothing the way. A glorified tour guide to start, in time he became a man Dickens could not do without. One of Roche's more delicate jobs involved scheduling stops at inns or even along the countryside so the members of the entourage could answer calls of nature shouted out when necessity demanded.

Roche led the merry travelers through Boulogne, Paris, Lyons, Avignon, Marseilles, and finally to Genoa, a destination Dickens chose after talking to his more well-traveled acquaintances.

Angus Fletcher, a short, overweight sculptor who had made a bust of Dickens and with whom Dickens had traveled through the highlands of Scotland, now lived in Genoa, and Dickens turned to Fletcher when he needed to find a residence. Dickens did not like the idea of taking a place sight unseen for an entire year, so he instructed Fletcher to lease a place for the summer in Albaro, a suburb two miles outside of Genoa, highly recommended by his well-traveled friends, with an additional nine-month extension available at Dickens' option. This caution would prove a wise move on Dickens' part.

Dickens was aghast at his first sight of Genoa. The crowded streets were grimy and reeked from unaccountable filth. The houses were dirty and randomly tumbled one atop another. The passages and byways of the city were more squalid and close than anything he ever encountered in London. The place smacked of nothing but dirt, discomfort, and decay. Outdoor vendors everywhere hawked lemons, oranges and even ice water. Nowhere did Dickens see the sunshine, brightness, and Italian glory he had expected.

The coach continued the two miles out of Genoa to the suburb of Albaro. His villa lay in a sequestered spot approached by lanes so very narrow the coach had to be measured before attempting a passage. The postilion fortunately managed to keep the traverse through these passages more successful and dignified than that of an old woman Dickens heard of whose coach wedged itself so tightly into one of the lanes the poor woman had to submit to the indignity of being hauled through one of the coach's little front windows like a traveling bag.

Finally, the coach stopped in front of a rank, dull, weedy courtyard, and Dickens learned that this miserable looking spot, the Villa di Bella Vista, or more popularly Villa Bagnerella after Bagnerella, the nearby butcher and proprietor, would be his home.

This place, too, filled Dickens with forlorn surprise, being as it seemed a citadel to ruin and neglect, and he felt immense relief knowing he had to spend no more than the three summer months in what he came to call the "pink jail." The garden was a shambles, the house itself cold and uninviting. The staircase leading to the grand *sala* on the second floor was cracked and the furniture ponderous, immovable, and uncomfortable. Though commodious, the house seemed as grim and bare a place as Dickens had ever seen or conceived of despite the beautiful vista it provided, overlooking as it did the Bay of Genoa.

Then they discovered the fleas. So many, in fact, poor Timber Doodle had to be shaved down to the skin to reduce his torment. In addition, swarms of mosquitoes kept

18

the family in despair. Flies buzzed everywhere. Dozens of scrawny cats prowled the grounds keeping the rats, thankfully, at bay. Lizards and scorpions basked in the sun and frogs gave gravel-throated concerts nightly.

The family settled in, though, and continued the Italian lessons they began in England while Dickens awaited the arrival of his writing gear—the desk knickknacks he needed before him as much as he needed pen, ink, and paper. While he waited, Dickens set out to find more suitable accommodations to move into as soon as his three months in Villa Bagnerello were up. Fletcher suggested Dickens speak with the same man he had spoken with when looking for a house in Albaro for Dickens—a Swiss banker by the name of Emile de la Rue.

Chapter Three

The family soon fell into a domestic routine. Barefoot townspeople appeared at the kitchen door every morning to sell fresh fruits and vegetables to the cook. The family ate breakfast at nine-thirty; dinner at four; bedtime around eleven. Charley, age seven, loved to take his brother Walter, age three, into the garden to watch the lizards scramble up the walls. Dickens added a piano to the house's limited amenities, hoping to expand the activities available for his children. He adamantly insisted, though, the family would not spend a day more than necessary in decrepit Villa Bagnerella, so Fletcher and he went to see Emile de la Rue some two weeks into his stay just before eleven o'clock in the morning.

Fletcher and Dickens negotiated the narrow pathways between the unkempt, overgrown villas of Albaro in a smaller carriage—riding a concession to Fletcher's girth—and entered the city.

"How are you getting on?" Fletcher asked.

"The sooner my mind is resolved on a new place to live, my getting on will be much improved," Dickens answered. Dickens saw the downcast look on Fletcher's face.

"No, no. Don't misunderstand me, Angus. You performed marvelously and did just what I asked. The villa has a great many things to recommend it—the rampant grapevines; the aroma of the orange and lemon trees; the rose petals strewn everywhere; and the sight of the bay. Did you know there's a path leading out through the garden and right down to the bay? And do you know the sea is actually visible from eleven different windows in the villa? The water is so blue! Why, I feel as if I could take a handful of that amazing blue, stare into it and have a great blue blank made of my intellect."

Fletcher smiled. "Not quite the thing for a novelist."

Dickens laughed. "There's only some editing and a Christmas book I need get done." Dickens laughed again. "I should have taken you into the kitchen when you arrived today. It's a grand show hearing the village vegetable sellers making offers in Genoese and waving their arms about as if they're planning to stab anyone nearby and my servants answering loudly in English as if they think the sellers deaf rather than Italian."

Both men laughed at the image.

When they neared the city, Dickens pointed to the sky with his right hand. "Look, Angus. Not an atom of smoke anywhere. Imagine breathing nothing but clean pure air for an entire year. I don't know whether my constitution will be up to it."

They soon entered the city's narrow streets, and Dickens looked around in silence at the poverty and the cracked buildings with peeling walls.

"How could they ever allow the city to deteriorate like this, Angus?"

Fletcher gave a shrug. "Politics. Lack of politics, leadership, guidance."

Dickens gazed in amazement at two naked children, a boy and a girl who looked about seven years old, playing with an old chair pulled from some vacated apartment. Watching the two children with an odd look of interest lay a gaunt, gray dog sprawled in a splash of shade. An old woman nearby, toothless and quite one of the ugliest creatures Dickens had ever seen—a hag straight from the brewing cauldrons of *Macbeth,* he later told his wife—shook her fist at him, and disappeared up an alley strewn with filth and garbage from the surrounding houses.

Dickens looked at Fletcher, who merely shrugged.

"Does every country have conditions like this?" Dickens asked, not expecting an answer. "I thought it might only be London. Good lord, Angus, look at them."

Three blind beggars were lolling in the shade taking turns crying out for alms. As Dickens and Fletcher drove by, a strong looking man without legs on a little go-cart joined the beggars. Dickens stared a moment and began to laugh. Fletcher looked at him in puzzlement.

"The legless man," Dickens pointed, shaking his head in mirth. "He looks as if he has sunk into the ground up to his middle, or has come part way up a flight of cellar steps to speak to somebody."

"Really, Charles," Fletcher chided.

Dickens wiped his eye and shook his head. "Sorry, Angus. Can't help it. It's the way my mind works. Oh," Dickens said, shaking and composing himself. "At any rate, how did you meet this de la Rue?"

"Through his wife. She's English. Augusta Spencer was her name. Someone introduced me to her in London some years ago, and we happened upon each other again here. They entertain, the de la Rues, and knowing I live here, she offered an invitation. Dropping your name and our Scottish adventures into the conversation didn't hurt, either."

Dickens rolled his eyes. "And him? What do you know about him?"

Fletcher took a breath. Dickens had been the same way on their tour of Scotland. Question after question. Wanting to know everything about everything. "From a very rich family. Banking, you know. I heard he was quite the roué in his younger days. He's, I believe, thirty-seven, thirty-eight now. Wife's some ten years younger. Quite lovely. You'll like her."

They had reached the Via de Campe and turned right. Suddenly, the air filled with the jangling of church bells.

"I never saw a city so in love with its bells," Dickens remarked with some asperity. He detested unnecessary noise, especially when working. "When I begin my story, I'm going to have to pause for five minutes every hour to compose myself after these dingling eruptions."

"We are in a city of churches, Charles," Fletcher explained.

"I know. I know."

The offices of the de la Rue banking interests were in a building mid-block. Fletcher led Dickens into the building and smiled at Dickens' amazement at seeing a bakery operating on the ground floor even though he had already commented to Dickens that Genoa was a city of noble residences crammed with miscellaneous occupants. The two men climbed the stairs to the second floor. Fletcher led the way into a large office lined with bookcases and wooden desks full of file drawers.

"Monsieur de la Rue is expecting us," Fletcher said in Italian to a young man seated at a small desk near the open window.

The young man rose and entered another door. In a moment he returned and told Dickens and Fletcher to go in.

A tall, handsome man neatly dressed in a trim gray suit, gray waistcoat, and white shirt sat behind an enormous desk. He smoothed his black hair, rose, and smiled.

"Ah, Angus."

"Emile, this is Charles Dickens. Charles, Emile de la Rue."

De la Rue circled his desk and extended his hand toward Dickens.

In French-accented English he welcomed his famous visitor. "Mr. Dickens, this is indeed an honor. Your name is known throughout all of Italy."

Dickens accepted the compliment with a smile and shook de la Rue's hand. "Thank you. You're very kind."

"Sit, please."

De la Rue motioned his guests to two starkly upright red leather chairs. He pulled a third over and completed the circle.

"I understand from Angus you are looking for new accommodations."

"Yes, Villa Bagnerello is quite lovely, but I don't believe it will be suitable for the colder weather."

"It is a shame you did not take the Doria Palace I first suggested to Angus. It is a magnificent home and only six miles from Genoa. I could have gotten it for you for forty pounds a year."

"That is my fault," Dickens explained, silently aggravated at the one-hundred-sixty-pounds-a year rate he paid for his current villa. "Angus followed my directions exactly. Friends in England told me Albaro was a beautiful spot. And it is. However, as I said, I'd prefer another place when colder weather sets in."

De la Rue smiled. "Yes, yes. I understand. I have many friends here in Genoa, and I will ask among them for you. I'm certain I can find something that will accommodate you. You have quite a large family group, I believe."

"Twelve, although it sometimes seems like a hundred and twelve."

De la Rue gave a slight laugh. "Excuse me, I'm being remiss. The presence of such a famous man has flustered me." De la Rue rose and went to his desk. He opened a bottom drawer and extracted an ornate wooden box. He brought it around and opened it in front of Dickens. Cigars.

"I have these sent from Havana. I think you will find them excellent."

"New to me," said Dickens.

"I predict you will never want to smoke a cigar made anywhere else after you smoke this one."

Dickens took a cigar and gestured his thanks.

"Angus?" offered de la Rue.

Fletcher took a cigar, and the three men worked over their cigars for a moment.

When clouds of smoke circled their heads, de la Rue said, "I hope you are not planning to write of us with the same disapproval you voiced about the Americans. You are planning a travel book, I presume."

25

"I am," Dickens informed him, impressed that de la Rue's mind ran toward an interest in his writing plans.

"I have read your *American Notes*. Is America as bad as all of that?"

"I'm afraid so. The constant spitting, I think, sums up America for me. Would you believe, at times my railroad car seemed to be carpeted with cotton balls from the constant expectoration?"

De la Rue's head bounced slightly with controlled laughter.

"Then perhaps it is a good thing you let your colonies have their way."

Dickens and Fletcher laughed politely.

"Genoa has its problems, believe me," said de la Rue, "but spitting..." He pronounced the word with infinite distaste. "...is not one of them."

Dickens indicated the cigar. "This is excellent."

"As promised," de la Rue said with a smile.

After a moment of silent smoking Fletcher said, "So, Emile, you will ask about for a new home for Mr. Dickens?"

"Yes, of course."

The three men rose.

"I will contact you, Mr. Dickens, as soon as I hear of something, and I hope we will meet again soon. I know my wife is eager to meet you. She is English, you know. And please, take these." He handed both Dickens and Fletcher three additional cigars each.

"You are most kind, Monsieur de la Rue," Dickens complimented. "And I do look forward to meeting your wife."

The three men walked to the office door.

"Until I hear from you then," said Dickens. Handshakes went round and Dickens and Fletcher left.

Chapter Four

Dickens' next-door neighbor at the Villa Bagnerello was the French Consul-General. The Consul and his English wife admired Dickens greatly. The Consul had even reviewed some of Dickens' novels in a French magazine. Taking advantage both of his position and proximity, and wanting to meet the great writer, the Consul invited the select of Genoa society to his villa in late August and naturally included Dickens and his wife among the invitees.

Dickens' writing materials had arrived in Genoa only two weeks before, and he had immediately set to work revising *Oliver Twist,* the only novel he retained the rights to at the moment, in preparation for Bradbury and Evans bringing it out in a single volume for the first time. Dickens hoped this little bit of work would also help nudge him toward solvency. As much as he had left it to Catherine to deal with Genoa society, even leaving the house when visitors dropped by, he happily anticipated the Consul's gathering. His knowing the Consul had written favorably about him played no small part in this happy anticipation.

Oddly enough, the Consul's villa was so shut away by its vineyard that, though right next door, to get there from the Villa Bagnerello was a mile's journey. On the final Friday evening in August, Dickens and his wife got into their carriage to make the short drive to the Consul's villa.

Dickens, dressed in a gray suit and glimmering black satin waistcoat complete with a red rose in his buttonhole, made certain to be fashionably late, hoping to assure a fuss upon his entrance. He succeeded. His appearance at the entrance to the grand *sala* stopped conversation and spun heads. He stood studiously oblivious to the attention, looking about and waiting for the Consul to welcome him. Being owned by a French Consul rather than a butcher apparently had a beneficial effect on a villa because the Consul's villa was in much better condition than his own. There were three tall windows in the *sala*, the rich red draperies pulled back to reveal a stunning view of the Bay of Genoa. Torches and candles lit the room brightly as finely dressed men and women, many holding wineglasses, tried with a feigned nonchalance to get a look at him. The floor was a beautiful swirl of tan and white marble, and the stairway to the grand *sala* had no cracks.

Dickens spotted the Consul bustling his way, a wide smile on his face, his hand outstretched in greeting. The Consul was a small man with a thin mustache and, at the moment, very eager brown eyes. In a thick accent he welcomed his guest.

"Monsieur Dickens, I am so happy you have accepted my invitation. You must let me take you and your wife around and introduce you."

This suited Dickens fine. Twenty minutes later the gathering returned to a semblance of what it had been before Dickens' arrival. Dickens left Catherine chatting with the Consul's English wife and helped himself to a glass of the local white wine, which, at a penny farthing a pint, had already become a great favorite of his. He had taken no more than a sip when he heard his name spoken by the one person he most hoped to see. Dickens turned to face Emile de la Rue.

De la Rue made a slight bow. "Welcome again to Genoa, Mr. Dickens. This time more formally."

"I hoped I might find you here, Monsieur de la Rue."

"I have good news for you. At least I hope it is good news."

Dickens lifted his wineglass slightly in a toast to de la Rue and waited for him to continue.

"There are rooms available in the Palazzo Peschiere. A Spanish duke lives in the room beneath what would be your apartments. He is a fine, quiet gentleman. Have you heard of it?"

"Palazzo Peschiere? The Palace of…Fishponds?"

"Yes." De la Rue brushed an invisible speck from the right side of his nose. "It is lovely and the rooms are available at the same price as the Doria Palace I mentioned the day you came to my office. Goldfish are provided."

Dickens smiled while doing a quick calculation. He would be saving nearly a hundred pounds over the course of his stay in Genoa.

De la Rue went on. "If you are free, I would be most happy to take you to see the Peschiere tomorrow afternoon. It is in Genoa, large enough for your family and quite fit for the winter."

"By all means. You have my thanks."

De la Rue gallantly waved off Dickens gratitude. "Your wife, I believe?" He indicated Catherine.

"Yes, let me introduce you." Dickens led de la Rue over to his wife. "Catherine, this is Emile de la Rue. He has found a lovely place for us to move into." After a few moments of polite conversation, Catherine returned to the Consul's wife, and Dickens and de la Rue helped themselves to another glass of wine.

"And where is your wife, Monsieur de la Rue? I've been looking forward to meeting her. English wives seem to be the fashion here in Genoa. So many men have chosen English brides." In a low conspiratorial voice Dickens added, "And rightly so, eh?"

The two men laughed.

"We must set to work to find one for Fletcher," Dickens went on.

"Oh, we must not set ourselves the task *impossibile.*"

The men laughed again.

Dickens waited to hear about Madame de la Rue, but de la Rue merely sipped his wine. He noticed Dickens' stare.

"Ah, yes. My wife. I must tell you she is an invalid, Mr. Dickens, and did not feel up to coming along this evening. Shortly after our marriage something struck her. I cannot even say what it is."

"I don't wish to pry, Monsieur de la Rue. If you'd rather not say..."

"No, no. I do not mean that. I mean it is very difficult to describe her symptoms."

Dickens' insatiable curiosity rose, and his expression clearly showed his interest. De la Rue continued.

"I say just after we were married she began to have these attacks...these movements of the face mostly, but not exclusively. 'Spasms' I believe is the correct word?"

Dickens nodded.

"These attacks sometime leave her helpless and seem generally to occur at night. She is often unable to sleep."

"This goes on every day, every night?"

"No, no, no. She has many good nights, but this malady is so unpredictable."

"Are there no competent doctors in Genoa?"

"They are at a loss what to do. Besides, she is reluctant to go to these doctors. They are not English, you see."

Dickens tilted his head thoughtfully. "Does she never get out?"

"Oh, she does. My, yes. She planned to be here this evening, but no more than an hour before we were to leave, she did not feel she could face all of these people. She and I are planning to be at the Marquis di Negri's gathering next Friday, though. Have you met the Marquis? He was a great friend of your Lord Byron."

Dickens nodded, his mind still fixed on Madame de la Rue. "Yes, the Consul introduced us."

"He is, I know, planning to invite you. You should be sure to put yourself in his way this evening."

"I will do so," said Dickens. The Consul appeared at his side.

"May I take Monsieur Dickens away, Emile?"

"My loss will be the gain of everyone else. I'm sure many people would like a word with Mr. Dickens. Be sure the Marquis has an opportunity to chat with him, Consul."

"Ah, yes." The Consul winked knowingly.

"Please give my best to your wife, Monsieur de la Rue. Tell her my wife and I look forward to meeting her."

Lowering his voice Dickens gave each man a sharp look and whispered, "Perhaps next Friday?"

The men laughed.

"On to *il Marchese*," Dickens cried, and off he went at the Consul's shoulder.

The grandeur of the Palazzo Peschiere stunned Dickens. It stood within the walls of Genoa (Genoa was a walled city which locked its gates at midnight) surrounded by beautiful gardens of its own, adorned with statues, vases, fountains, marble basins, terraces, walks of orange and lemon trees, and groves of roses and camellias, and of course, boasted the fishpond. The rooms were uniformly spacious, but Dickens was most impressed by the grand *sala*, some fifty feet in height with three large windows at the end overlooking the whole town of Genoa, the harbor, and the neighboring sea. The walls and ceiling of the *sala* were adorned with three hundred year old frescoes whose colors looked as fresh as the day they were painted. The remaining rooms opened off the *sala*, and everything Dickens saw pleased him. Where the Villa Bagnerello was dismal and barely habitable, the Palazzo Peschiere seemed bright, cheerful, lavish, and inviting. Dickens described it to his family as an enchanted palace in an Eastern story.

Dickens leased the Peschiere for October through June and offered his profuse thanks to Emile de la Rue. The two men looked forward to meeting again the following Friday evening at the Marquis di Negri's villa.

On Friday night, however, Dickens' wife stayed at

home to care for daughter Kate, who had developed a fever, so Dickens was driven alone to the Marquis' lavish villa, timing his entrance, as usual, with some specificity. As usual, he dressed to be noticed, tonight wearing a tan suit over a yellow waistcoat, a white rose in his lapel.

No sooner had Dickens entered the Marquis' grand *sala* than the very fat and very old Marquis approached him gushing, "Ah, Monsieur Dickens, an honor, an honor. Let me show you my home." The Marquis' home was indeed grand, but Dickens had grown a bit weary of looking at high-ceilinged, spacious rooms. He put as much enthusiasm as he could into his responses as the Marquis even took him outside for a tour of the grottoed walks under variegated lights that laced the fragrant, colorful gardens.

Back inside the brightly lit *sala* Dickens eased himself away from the Marquis, helped himself to some delicious chilled white wine, highly recommended by the Marquis, and searched the crowd. Standing before a fresco of angels wafting a serenely peaceful Mary to heaven stood Emile de la Rue, a young woman with bunched, shimmering black hair, dressed in a white gown by his side. The woman's hair sparkled as she turned her head to speak to the people around her, and Dickens saw she wore a tiara. De la Rue noticed Dickens, and his eyes widened in recognition and greeting. He put his hand on the young woman's shoulder, made a few more comments to the group of which he and she were a part, and then escorted the woman toward Dickens.

Dickens' eyes darted from de la Rue to the woman and back. The woman was lovely. She came up to de la

Rue's shoulder, and was slightly shorter than Dickens. Dickens inspected her a second time and their eyes held. She had sparkling blue eyes and an easy, natural smile. Her mouth was small and tending to round with a prominent upper lip that rose slightly in the middle. Her lips were quite red and resembled in Dickens' mind nothing so much as a delicate rose bud about to blossom.

"Monsieur Dickens, may I present my wife Augusta."

"Mr. Dickens." The woman smiled with a slight bow of the head.

"Madame de la Rue, my pleasure." Dickens bobbed his head once with gusto.

"It is such an honor to meet so famous a countryman."

"And I am delighted at meeting so beautiful a countrywoman."

"Oh, my." Madame de la Rue smiled. "And your wife?"

"Ah, little Kate, my daughter, has been feverish these past few days, and my wife is being nursemaid tonight."

"Oh, I'm so sorry. I looked forward to meeting her. I've heard so much about her from the Consul's wife." The Consul's wife and Catherine Dickens had exchanged visits during the week after their introduction at the Consul's party.

"Give her our best, please," said Madame de la Rue. "And I do hope your daughter feels better soon."

The Marquis bounced ploddingly into the group. "Emile, Emile, you must meet my wife's cousin, newly arrived from England. A banker like yourself."

"Darling?" said de la Rue to his wife.

She smiled. "You go on. Mr. Dickens will entertain

me?" She pursed her lips to make her statement a question.

"It will be an honor."

De la Rue and the Marquis strode off across the room. Dickens and Augusta de la Rue looked at each other, Dickens immersing himself in her shining blue eyes. She looked down.

When she glanced back at him she said, "I hear from our friend Angus your first impressions of Genoa were anything but positive."

Dickens shrugged. "My first look at the city did provide something of a shock. It hasn't been very well kept up. My own villa is a dilapidated sty, but don't mention it to Angus. He chose the villa, but he did no more than I asked him to do. And the poverty on the streets here rivals our own London. While walking yesterday in the city I passed what looked like five bundles of locomotive rags. It turned out to be a mother and her four children. For one moment I felt as if I'd never left home. Another person, a woman, inspected the hair of a child for lice right out on the street. Is anything done for these people here?"

Madame de la Rue shook her head slightly, drew her lips together thoughtfully, and said, "Are there no prisons? Are there no workhouses?"

Dickens gaped for a moment. Madame de la Rue touched him on the arm and gave a small laugh. "Don't take me seriously, Mr. Dickens. I regularly give money to the poor, and I donate to the church, which I trust does its duty toward the poor."

Dickens smiled, all thoughts of the poor melting away. "You've read my book."

"Of course. I've read all of your books. They are wonderful. I have my sister send me the chapters as they come out. She lives in London. It's only been a month since the final chapters of *Martin Chuzzlewit* reached me. America." She gave a small, theatrical shudder. "Are you writing while you're here in Genoa?"

Dickens loved for people to take an interest in his interests, especially in his writing. His words came faster. "I'm planning a Christmas book. The idea I have will I hope strike the heaviest blow I can wield in favor of the poor. I've not begun it yet. I'm still searching for a framework, a title..."

Suddenly, Madame de la Rue's eyebrows flicked twice up her forehead, and the left corner of her mouth pulled backwards three times. The movements were so unexpected and Dickens gaze so intense as he described his coming Christmas book, his surprise froze both his tongue and his expression.

"Oh, I'm sorry. This strikes me at times," Madame de la Rue explained softly.

"My apologies for my reaction. It was...I..." Rarely at a loss for words, Dickens nonetheless found himself befuddled.

Madame de la Rue touched his arm again. "Think nothing of it." Again her eyebrows shot upwards and the left corner of her mouth pulled back twice. "I hardly know it's happening myself."

"A new malady since you've been married, your husband tells me?" Dickens prodded, his focus now shifted to the woman's explanation.

"Yes. Usually it's no more than what you've seen."

37

"Usually?"

Madame de la Rue took a breath. "Would you like to get some air, Mr. Dickens?"

"Yes, I would."

Madame de la Rue led him down the grand stairway and out onto one of the grottoed walks under the rainbow of lights.

"A lovely night," she sighed and inhaled deeply. "The aroma of the breeze..."

Dickens waited to hear more.

"You seem quite interested in my health, Mr. Dickens." She turned a smiling face toward him.

"I hope I'm not offending..."

Madame de la Rue waved her hand slightly. "To tell you the truth I'm glad to have an Englishman to talk to about it. An intelligent Englishman."

Dickens did not respond.

"Sometimes I can barely sleep, the dreams are so bad."

"Dreams?"

"Sometimes these spasms are so severe I slip into and out of consciousness. There are things in my dreams then..."

Madame de la Rue's mouth began to twitch repeatedly, and she seemed to drift into a strange preoccupation.

"Madame, please. Don't speak any more of it. I see how it distresses you."

Madame de la Rue looked at Dickens as if seeing him for the first time. She took a deep breath.

"No, no. I won't. Please forget I mentioned it. Let's

just circle the garden and return to the party."

Dickens and Madame de la Rue walked, talking of England, as they circled the garden and retraced their steps inside and up the stairs to the grand *sala*. Emile de la Rue waited there.

"Ah, here you are, my dear. Come, there are people you must say hello to."

Both Augusta and Emile de la Rue made their excuses to Dickens and walked off.

Dickens mingled with the other guests for the rest of the evening, hoping for another opportunity to speak with Madame de la Rue. He wanted the opportunity to tell her about his good friend Dr. John Elliotson, whom he knew for a fact had treated patients with symptoms like she had.

Late in the evening Augusta de la Rue approached him.

"So sorry to have been ignoring you," she said with an ingratiating smile, "but my husband has so many business acquaintances and I must, it seems, meet and chat with them all."

"Your husband is a busy and important man," Dickens responded, hoping to find a way back to the topic of her malady.

Madame de la Rue gave an odd twist of her head. "Don't you live outside the city, Mr. Dickens?"

"Why yes. In Albaro."

"Well, it is near midnight. If you don't leave now, you'll never get outside the gates in time."

Dickens pulled his watch from his pocket. He had been so intent on speaking a second time with Madame de la

Rue he had ignored the passage of time. And he had absent-mindedly ordered his coach back well past midnight.

"My lord. You're right." The prospect of explaining to his wife why he had not come home all night, and her nursing a sick child, loomed unattractively before Dickens' eyes.

Madame de la Rue smiled and pointed to her right. There the Marquis laughed heartily at something one of his guests said to him.

"Yes. Thanks. It's been a pleasure. Good night." He rushed over to the Marquis and made a quick, grateful acknowledgment of his hospitality. Dickens hurried to the stairs and rushed out into the night.

Chapter Five

At a distance from the Marquis' villa compatible with dignity, Dickens began to run as hard as he could along the Strada Sevra, a newly constructed street. The ground he raced over was uneven and led downhill. Out of nowhere Dickens felt a stunning crack across his breast. Unlit and unattended, a pole fastened across the street breast high slammed into him and he spun headlong over it. He landed, rolling forcefully in the dusty road. Dickens lay stunned, his clothing shredded in places.

He got to his feet and, after a brief moment to be certain he'd broken no bones, he hurried on, intent on making it through the midnight gate. Only a few steps outside the gate he heard the midnight chimes of Genoa sound in various church towers of the town. Safely on his way home now, Dickens paused a moment to listen. Chimes. The chimes at midnight. Chimes, of course! He could build his Christmas story on the chimes. Doubly relieved at not having killed himself in his haste to get home and at having gotten an inspiration albeit it at a most bizarre moment for his story, Dickens strode the two miles to Albaro, though at something slower than his usual four miles per hour pace.

The next morning he felt miserable. Either the blow he had taken when he smashed into the pole or the rattling he had received when he hit the ground had reawakened the pain in his left kidney he had experienced off and on since childhood. Through Dickens' mind passed the memory of

Bob Fagin, one of his young co-workers in the blacking factory of cursed and undisclosed memory, applying hot water bottles to him at age twelve when the agony set in.

He lay in bed, breathing shallowly, trying to ignore the pain. Catherine, who had risen early, bustled into the room.

"What did you do to yourself last night?" she asked, a sprinkling of disdain in her voice. "Your clothes are all torn and dirty. Did you crawl home?" She held his ripped suit jacket before him.

"An accident," he explained wearily. He mentioned his pain.

Catherine's voice softened some. "Well, you just lie still today. I'll have Georgy fix you some hot compresses."

Dickens nodded, in no mood or condition to argue.

The warm compresses kept coming during the day, and by the time Dickens had finished a late afternoon meal in bed, he felt much better. He rose and dressed slowly, planning to go no farther than the garden, when Catherine walked into the bedroom.

"You have a visitor. A Madame de la Rue. She has come with her maid."

"You've seen her?"

"No, Anne brought me her card." Anne was Mrs. Dickens' personal maid.

"I'm sure she's here to see us both. I met her at the Marquis' last night, and she asked for you. You met her husband, you recall. She passed along her best for little Kate. I'm not at all surprised she's decided to visit."

"You weren't expecting her? I see you're dressed."

"I was on my way to sit in the garden. Come, we shouldn't keep her waiting."

Dickens and his wife met Augusta de la Rue in the entry room off the main hall. After the appropriate introductions, the three of them proceeded into the garden. Catherine reported on little Kate's health, Dickens reported on his accident, and somehow his kidney ailment found its way into the conversation.

Madame de la Rue said, "We both have our health shortcomings then, I see."

"Both?" Catherine queried.

Madame de la Rue explained her malady to Kate, Dickens listening closely for any added information but hearing far fewer details than the night before. Madame de la Rue omitted telling Kate about her odd dreams.

Georgina, Catherine's younger sister, appeared and informed Catherine her daughter was asking for her. Catherine excused herself and, with Georgina, went to tend to the sick girl.

The eyes of Dickens and Madame de la Rue followed the departing women. When they had no other choice, they looked at each other.

"You do look somewhat pale, Mr. Dickens. I hope you will rest. I called to invite you and your wife to our home later this month, the third Friday. A small dinner for friends. Nothing like the open houses of the Consul and the Marquis, although both will be invited, along with the esteemed Governor of Genoa. Have you met him?"

Dickens nodded. "Yes, yes I have. Of course my wife and I will be there. May I ask you something?"

The corner of Madame de la Rue's mouth twitched twice. She gave an odd sideways nod of her head and waited.

"You didn't mention your dreams to my wife. Was there a reason?"

"You are very sharp, Mr. Dickens. Please forget I ever mentioned them." Madame de la Rue glanced down guiltily. "Nor have I told my husband."

"Not of the dreams?"

The woman shook her head and looked at Dickens. "I don't know why I mentioned them to you. For some reason I cannot bring myself to reveal those dreams to him, even though there isn't much to reveal. I..." She stopped talking.

"You're under no obligation to tell *me* about them, I assure you."

"I know. I know. Ah, your wife is returning. If you will keep my secret...?"

Dickens made a quick move with his right hand to indicate agreement.

Dickens apprised Catherine of the de la Rues' invitation, and Catherine responded with proper gratitude. The visit ended soon after. Madame de la Rue insisted Dickens stay in the garden and rest rather than see her out. Dickens complied.

After going over what Madame de la Rue had told him about her dreams and being unable to make any more of it than he already had, he turned his mind to his Christmas story. He had written Forster just the other day about his troubles in starting the story without first finding a proper title for it. He called for pen and paper and wrote a one-sentence letter to Forster. The letter read, "We have heard

THE CHIMES at midnight, Master Shallow!" He laughed as he handed the letter back to his servant for mailing. Forster would be certain to get his joke.

The de la Rues postponed their dinner from the third to the final Friday in September. The note Dickens received omitted the reason, and Dickens wondered whether Madame de la Rue's condition caused the postponement. The week following this dinner the Dickens family would make their two-mile move from the Villa Bagnerello to the Palazzo Peschiere, and the family found the respite in planning and packing provided by the dinner party most welcome.

The de la Rues lived in Genoa on the top floor of the Palazzo Brignole Rosso, a building not far from the office where Dickens first visited de la Rue. Like the Consul's home and the Marquis' home, the de la Rues' home was an island of elegance amid the squalor of Genoa. Ornately framed paintings hung on the walls. Richly detailed, hand-woven carpets covered the floor of each room. Two additional servants—four total—had been hired for the night as well as an additional cook. The dining table was set with beautiful china plates rimmed with decorative and intricately etched grapevines, and faceted, glittering crystal glasses stood alongside, waiting to be filled with the delicious local wines. Above the dining table an ornate crystal chandelier hung directly over a floral centerpiece composed entirely of camellias.

Dickens wore his bright red waistcoat and his black suit complete with a red rose buttonhole. Catherine wore her lavender gown. By now a somewhat familiar figure among this society, Dickens' entrance caused little stir. Emile de la

Rue greeted each guest upon arrival. "Mr. Dickens, welcome to my home. Mrs. Dickens." After assuring de la Rue he'd had an uneventful two-mile carriage ride and being reminded by de la Rue that come next week he would be a full-fledged Genoese, Dickens moved off, leaving his wife, as had become routine, in the hands of the French Consul's wife. Dickens spotted Madame de la Rue speaking with the Governor. He watched as her eyebrows and the corner of her mouth danced more than Dickens had ever seen. He frowned and wondered if a specific cause or certain state of mind induced these spasms in the woman.

Madame de la Rue noticed him and nodded while she continued to speak with the Governor. Dickens, satisfied Madame had discovered his arrival, wandered away to find a glass of wine. He gazed out over the city from a window when he felt a touch on his arm.

Dickens turned. "Madame de la Rue."

"I see you are moving much better than when last we met." She smiled, her gaze calm and happy, her eyes sparkling and a Genoese bay blue.

"Oh, yes, yes. That's passed. The accident caused it. I have worse infirmities to worry about, I assure you."

"Really?" The calm and happy gaze changed. A look of concerned interest settled in her eyes.

Dickens hoped his describing his occasional attacks of facial neuralgia would induce the woman to describe her own infirmity in more detail.

"I had no idea being a famous author brought on such precarious health," she said thoughtfully when Dickens had finished his litany of aches and pains.

"No. My youthful days, something about them has left me like this."

Madame de la Rue commenced a strange movement of her head, once, twice, thrice, bending it sharply toward her right shoulder and then upright again. She looked back at Dickens.

"I've had a very hard week."

"Your postponed dinner...?"

"Yes. Sometimes and unaccountably I feel so fearful...I don't know what of...so fearful I cannot bring myself to leave home."

Dickens readily anticipated pursuing the topic but couldn't. "I see your husband beckoning you."

"Oh, the English Consul has arrived."

"I've been looking forward to meeting him."

"I'll bring him over." She excused herself and went to her husband.

She had had a bad week, Dickens pondered. He'd wanted to suggest to her tonight that she describe her malady to him in detail so he could write Elliotson in London for advice. Elliotson was a master at these kinds of things. Perhaps even he himself...

Suddenly, a stir of activity caught Dickens' eye, and he saw Madame de la Rue lying on the floor wracked with tremors, almost like an epileptic fit. He rushed over.

Emile de la Rue knelt over her. "Darling, darling." He looked into the crowd gathered about him. "Please, help me get her to her bedroom."

Dickens and two other men stepped forward. They

gently lifted Madame de la Rue to her feet.

"Stay away. Stay away," the woman moaned. Dickens noted her eyes were closed, and she addressed no one in particular.

The men, Dickens included, gently guided Madame de la Rue out of the room. De la Rue opened a door, and the men took the lady into a bedroom. They sat her on the bed, and Dickens watched her closely.

"Stay away," she whispered once more and her eyes opened. She looked around groggily until she focused on her husband's face. "Oh, Emile."

"I am here, darling. I am here. Gentlemen, leave us. She will be fine. I will care for her, and our dinner will go on."

Reluctantly, Dickens followed the other two men from the room.

The dinner did go on but under the somber cloud of Madame de la Rue's attack. She did not appear at the table or any time thereafter. The party dissolved earlier than it would have otherwise, and the guests left, each expressing appropriate concern to Emile de la Rue. Dickens and his wife rode home, Dickens showing his wife the offending midnight pole on the way.

The next few days encompassed the move to the Palazzo Peschiere and were a whirl of packing, unpacking, exploration and delight. Once settled in his new home Dickens dedicated the month of October to completing his Christmas book, *The Chimes*, and on the third of November at half-past two in the afternoon, he wrote "The End" to his manuscript. Other than nighttime walks about

Genoa, the writing had been his only activity. He had even denied entrance to the Governor of Genoa, who called to pay his respects and to invite the Dickens family to a gathering at his palazzo, by having his wife explain he was engaged on a book and could not be disturbed. The Governor subsequently took on a proprietary interest in Dickens' literary progress, telling everyone at his gathering, as if they did not know any better, "the great poet" was writing a book and should be left alone until he was ready to receive visitors.

Dickens had gauged the completion of his manuscript accurately. He wanted to reciprocate the hospitality he had been shown in Genoa before he left on November sixth for a tour of northern Italy. He also planned a trip to England to read his new story to John Forster and other friends whom Forster would gather together. He thought *The Chimes* the most powerful story he had ever written, and he could not wait to show off what he had done. On a more mundane note, he also needed to see the story proofs through publication. He planned to be back in Genoa before Christmas.

To accomplish his intended reciprocation he had set Friday, November 5 as the date for a dinner at his new and elegant palazzo. He had sent invitations to the French and English Consuls, the Governor, Angus Fletcher, the Marquis de Negri, and Sir George Crawford, an English banker then visiting Genoa. He also sent an invitation to the de la Rues accompanied by a personal note of invitation to Madame de la Rue. She responded with a personal note of her own, promising to make every attempt to attend the dinner.

All Dickens could do now was hope she would show

up.

Taking a cue from the de la Rues, Dickens hired three waiters and would have hired an additional cook if the Governor of Genoa had not already offered the use of his own two cooks, a municipal courtesy extended to Genoa's famous visitor. Dickens, however, insisted on overseeing everything from the purchase of the fish to the folding of the napkins.

As a special recompense for all of the help Emile de la Rue had given him in finding suitable places to live, Dickens asked the de la Rues to arrive at five-thirty, an hour before the time he told the other guests.

Dickens and his wife took the couple into the garden, where a few late-blooming roses and camellias lingered. After a brief discussion about the wonders of the Palazzo Peschiere, Dickens said, "Monsieur de la Rue, Madame, I had a second purpose in mind when I asked you to come here before the others; a second purpose besides offering my heartfelt gratitude to you both for your many kindnesses." Dickens had plotted his approach carefully. He had not shared his scheme with Catherine, and he could feel her stare. He did, though, want her to hear his suggestion first hand.

Looking straight at Emile de la Rue he continued. "I believe I may be able to help your wife, perhaps even cure her of her attacks and her sleepless nights." He trusted his using the innocuous term "sleepless nights" would both keep de la Rue in the dark about Madame's secret and indicate to Madame herself his promise to rid her of her dreams.

De la Rue straightened himself and looked at his wife.

"What do you mean, Mr. Dickens?" de la Rue asked,

his eyebrows contracting into a straight line as he gazed back at Dickens.

"In London there is a doctor, a very good friend of mine. His name is John Elliotson. He has achieved wonderful cures of patients with symptoms similar to your wife's. I have seen him work. I have read of his cures."

"What is his secret?" de la Rue asked, not entirely taking Dickens forthright manner in all seriousness.

"Mesmerism. He uses mesmerism. He has given his patients new lives with his treatments. I have seen it. I can vouch for it."

"Mesmerism!" de la Rue intoned, eyebrows rising.

"Let me explain." Dickens took the next fifteen minutes explaining the concepts behind animal magnetism and the methods employed by its practitioners.

When Dickens finished, he sat back and kept his eyes on Emile de la Rue. De la Rue drew a deep breath. "I scarcely know what to say. Augusta?"

Augusta nodded slowly. "I believe Mr. Dickens can help, Emile. I don't know much about this Doctor Elliotson, but I have heard his name. He is quite reputable."

Dickens sensed an opening and addressed Madame de la Rue. "I would ask your leave to acquaint Dr. Elliotson with your symptoms and get his advice. Tomorrow I'm leaving Genoa for some six weeks. I will be in London in early December. I would write to Dr. Elliotson now and see him when I reach London. When I return to Genoa, I will follow the doctor's advice and begin treatment."

"You!" de la Rue exclaimed.

"I am a capable mesmerist, sir." Dickens now told the

story of meeting Elliotson and being trained by him. He told of his successful attempts to mesmerize his wife some two years before in America and of inducing what at first was a frightening but then a controllable mesmeric trance; of mesmerizing his sister-in-law Georgina and others at first simply for entertainment's sake, but subsequently to alleviate their illnesses. "I am certain I can help," he concluded.

Emile de la Rue looked at Mrs. Dickens.

"What he says is true," she reported grudgingly. "My husband can do the things he claims."

Augusta de la Rue answered before her husband could. "Yes, Mr. Dickens. Yes. I want very much *to* be helped."

"Monsieur de la Rue?" Dickens asked more stiffly than he meant to.

"Why...why certainly. If you can help Augusta in any way, then you must, of course."

"Excellent. Then I will do as I said. I will write Elliotson before we leave Genoa. If I could have a few moments alone with Madame tonight so I can be certain my letter is accurate..."

"Certainly," Augusta de la Rue answered.

Georgina appeared and informed the group the other guests had begun to arrive, and everyone left the garden to join the new arrivals.

After dinner Dickens invited Augusta de la Rue into the garden again. As they passed beneath the windows where the dinner had taken place, Dickens glanced up and saw Catherine looking down. Dickens disdained to give notice of his wife's attention and continued out of sight of the window.

He led Madame de la Rue through the large garden to the fishpond where they sat on wooden benches.

Dickens did not hesitate. "Madame, I need to know details of your dreams. On my honor I will keep what you tell me confidential, save my telling it to Dr. Elliotson."

Augusta de la Rue looked at Dickens.

Dickens sensed her reluctance and tried to reassure her. "Let me first say that it is a most astonishing coincidence that I have never in my life, whatever projects I may have determined on otherwise—never begun a book or begun anything of interest to me, or done anything of importance to me, but it was on a Friday. Why, I was born on a Friday, you know. You and I first met on a Friday. I purposely planned tonight's dinner for a Friday so I could make the offer I've made you on a Friday. It is a good omen. I know it is. But I would like to ask you a few things, if I may."

Madame de la Rue nodded and stared into the dark water of the fishpond.

"These attacks—when did they begin?"

She turned toward Dickens. "Two weeks, a month, after Emile and I married, nearly ten years ago."

Dickens shook his head in sympathy. "For so long? And the frequency of these attacks?"

"Oh, every week in a minor way such as you saw the first night we met. I scarcely know it happens."

"And attacks like the one at your home?"

She looked down. "There is no telling. Sometimes not for months; then sometimes I go nights on end without sleep."

"And the dreams?"

Augusta de la Rue astonished Dickens by reaching out her hand and clasping his.

"They are awful. So dark and frightening. Something...someone is in my dreams. Threatening me. Coming after me. Oh, I can't. I can't."

Dickens' stomach dropped in fear as Augusta de la Rue's head began to quiver and bounce toward her right shoulder.

"I will ask no more, Madame. No more. I have heard enough."

Dickens' fingers hurt from the pressure of the woman's hand. He put his other hand atop their two and gently stroked. In a quiet, even voice he said, "There will soon come a time when I will need you to trust me absolutely, Augusta."

At the sound of her first name the pressure on Dickens' hand lightened.

"Tell me you will trust me. I can help you. By God, I know I can help you."

Madame de la Rue slowly moved her head upright.

"Breathe deeply. Breathe evenly, Augusta. Tell me that you will trust me."

The woman's eyes closed. As Dickens watched the rise and fall of her breathing, she moved her head slowly and affirmatively.

"Yes, Charles." Her eyes opened. The touch of their hands had become normal. For the first time Dickens noticed how soft and warm her hand was. He gently stroked her long fingers with his top hand.

"Yes, Charles. I do trust you. I will do whatever you say." Her mouth twitched slightly.

Dickens released her hand.

"Then we understand each other, Augusta."

"Yes, Charles."

Dickens rose and helped the woman to her feet. "Be assured, I will do all in my power to help you."

Saying little else they walked back the way they had come and returned to the party.

Having achieved what he had set out to achieve put Dickens in excellent spirits for the rest of the night. He even sang some of the comic songs—"The Cat's Meat Man" twice by popular demand—his father taught him as a child, a talent of his in which his father had taken great pride. By the party's end Monsieur de la Rue was no longer Monsieur de la Rue but Emile, and Mr. Dickens was no longer Mr. Dickens but Charles.

The following day Dickens and his faithful courier Louis Roche left Genoa, his family remaining behind. They visited Parma, Modena, Bologna, Venice, Padua, Verona, Mantua, and Milan. On Sunday, December first, he arrived in London. On the second he read *The Chimes* to Forster, Thomas Carlyle, his brother Fred, and a half-dozen other notable friends and basked in their praise and their tears.

On December third he and Dr. John Elliotson dined alone. On the fourth he gave another reading of *The Chimes* to a second group Forster gathered. He spent two long days with Bradbury and Evans seeing to the publication of *The Chimes*—without the costly color illustrations which had cut into the profits of *A Christmas Carol*.

Sunday night, December eighth, found Dickens back on the road, and by December twenty-second he had returned to Genoa, ready to resume his Italian sojourn. Soon to be added to the routine of his domestic life, however, were near daily visits to the Palazzo Brignole Rosso to mesmerize Augusta de la Rue.

Chapter Six

On Monday, two days before Christmas and Dickens' first full day back from England, a note from Emile de la Rue arrived at his breakfast table. The note read:

"Charles,
My wife has suffered greatly since you left. I have never seen her like this. Have you brought a remedy? Can you visit as soon as possible?
Emile."

Dickens finished off a slice of ham, explained his destination to an unresponsive Catherine, and put himself to rights. Satisfied with his appearance, he briskly walked the short distance between the Peschiere and the Brignole Rosso. Emile de la Rue himself opened the apartment door.

"Oh, Charles. Welcome, welcome. I hoped you could come." De la Rue closed the door behind Dickens and led him by the arm toward the same bedroom where Augusta de la Rue had been helped the night she collapsed at the dinner party.

"Your trip, Charles? How was it?"

"Deuce take my trip. Tell me about your wife."

They paused outside the bedroom door. De la Rue kept his hand on Dickens' arm. Dickens waited, keenly attentive.

"She has had so little sleep. Her nights have been fearful. Not until the afternoon does Augusta seem to be settled enough to rest, and only then, I fear, because she is so exhausted by what she suffered the night before."

"Has she been eating?"

"Dinner has generally been a quiet time, but she's taken very little at other times. As the night deepens the attacks begin."

"Go on."

De la Rue heaved a heavy sigh. "She becomes someone other than herself. There is fear in her eyes. Her movements...her trembling...it frightens me. She's cried out on occasion."

"Saying what?"

De la Rue shrugged and gestured to indicate the lack of sense in his wife's ravings.

"How is she today?"

"The days have fallen into much of a pattern. Mornings, she lies in bed as now, exhausted but unable to sleep. You will see a change in her, I'm afraid."

Dickens looked toward the bedroom door.

"May I go in?" he asked.

"Yes. Frida and Giovanni are nearby if you need them." Frida and Giovanni were the two de la Rue servants. "Giovanni will come and get me from the office if necessary. Let me take you in."

Dickens stopped de la Rue. "You'll be going to your office, then?"

"Yes. Augusta's poor health has become our daily routine and today, unfortunately, is a day like every other.

Generally, though, she improves as the day goes on, but as the night progresses..." De la Rue gestured helplessly.

Dickens nodded. He had been prepared to explain to de la Rue why he needed to be alone with Augusta—how the powers of mesmerism required an undisturbed attachment to the patient. He said only, "Yes, Emile, go to your office. It's better I work with your wife with nothing to distract her."

"You believe you can help her, then?"

"I know I can."

De la Rue opened the bedroom door.

Augusta de la Rue turned toward them at the sound. The woman's face looked sallow and thinner, her eyes dull and full of weariness. Her hair hung limply across the pillow and over the edge of the bed. Dickens rigidly kept the shock he felt to himself.

"Oh, Mr. Dickens." She managed to sit up. "I hate to have you see me this way."

"Charles came at once, darling," de la Rue told her.

Augusta smiled. "You are very kind, Mr. Dickens."

Dickens moved a chair to the bedside. Before he sat he turned back to de la Rue and stared at him.

"Ah, yes. Augusta, I will be at the office. I leave you in good hands. Giovanni will come for me if necessary. Help her, Charles. Please." De la Rue walked to the opposite side of the bed, leaned over, and kissed his wife. He left the room and closed the door behind him.

Augusta turned quickly to Dickens. "Oh, Charles, I have been so unwell."

"The dreams?"

"Yes, yes. Someone is in my dreams. He won't let

me sleep." The left side of her face began to twitch. Her eyes closed and opened wearily. The corner of her mouth jumped. Dickens took her hand.

"Augusta, you must trust me. Absolutely."

Dickens could see there would be little problem in extracting trust from his patient. Eager dependence already shone from her eyes.

"Look at me. Listen to me." Dickens stroked her hand slowly, from the wrist down to the tips of her fingers. "You need rest. I need to make you stronger. We will lay to rest this accursed phantom. Trust me, we will. But you must believe in me." Augusta began to answer, but Dickens held up his hand. "Shhh. Your words are not necessary now. I promise I will come to you whenever you need me, day or night. I will be here every morning, just as I am here today, and every morning I will see to it you rest. No, don't look away. You must see in my eyes my concern for you. Do not look away from me." He continued to stroke her hand, and kept his voice in "an assured and assuring monotone," as Elliotson had recommended. "You are going to feel tired. More tired than you have ever felt."

Dickens could feel Augusta losing herself in his eyes as if she were falling into a pool of warm and soothing water. He recalled the power he felt when he read *The Chimes* to Forster and the others. When he looked up from his reading and made eye contact with one of his audience, that person could not look away from him. Dickens knew the profound authority of his visual ray.

"The problem will be your eyelids. You will not be able to keep them open. They will be pulled shut by tremendously heavy weights. You will find it impossible to remain awake."

Dickens felt a nervous tremor run through him as Augusta's eyelids fluttered.

"I will force you to sleep and to rest. When you are stronger, we will expel the phantom that haunts you. Listen to me closely, Augusta. There is a state between waking and sleeping where a person can experience more in five minutes than in a month of dreams. You will eventually tell me what you experience when you are in that state. The phantom will come to fear us. It will come to fear you." Augusta's eyelids closed, fluttered open, and closed again. "For now I want only for you to rest. The phantom will not return today. You will rest, and you will become strong."

Augusta's head rolled to the right side, away from Dickens. He continued to stroke her hand and repeat things he had already said to her. Augusta's fingers relaxed in his grasp. Her breathing grew strong and steady. Scarcely breathing himself, he laid Augusta's hand down on the counterpane and sat watching over her as she slept. Fifteen minutes later, assured her sleep was deep and sound, Dickens rose and left the room.

He sought out Giovanni and in his best Italian said, "Your mistress is resting. Do not enter the room. Keep the house quiet. Ask Monsieur de la Rue to write me as soon as he comes home and tell me how Madame is."

Giovanni understood and Dickens left.

Catherine asked no questions about his visit to the de la Rues, and Dickens chose not to favor her with a report unless she did so. He spent the day catching up on correspondence that had reached the Peschiere during his absence, but as darkness drew near, his thoughts returned to Augusta de la Rue. He tried to do some reading in the room he had made his office, but he could not concentrate. In his mind he reviewed everything Dr. Elliotson had told him. Cure the symptoms. Find the cause. The cause. Augusta's phantom. What could it be? What did it mean? It would take time to learn the truth.

When the anticipated note from the Brignole Rosso came, Dickens took it back into his office and opened it. It read:

> *Charles,*
> *You worked wonders. My wife slept much of the day and feels far better as a consequence. She is now dressing for dinner.*
> *I pray that this result continues. How can we be certain it does? Many, many thanks.*
> *Emile.*

Dickens thought a moment and composed a reply. It read:

> *Emile,*
> *Your letter is exactly the news I had hoped for. I will, with your permission, visit Madame each morning for the near future and provide a mesmeric treatment to enable her to rest, if one is needed. Do not hesitate to call*

on me, day or night, if I can be of service.

Charles.

He sealed the note and sent his servant with it on the short trip to the de la Rues. Immensely pleased with the results of his morning, Dickens sought his wife out to inform her.

"Dinner will be at six," she reported when Dickens found her overseeing the cook in the kitchen.

"Kate, I've received a note from Emile. It seems I worked something of a miracle this morning with Madame de la Rue. I showed you this morning's note. Read this. It's just arrived. I enabled her to rest comfortably all day."

"Did you? It must be a great comfort to them both." His wife continued to bustle about, ignoring the proffered note.

"Yes, yes. No doubt. I'm going to visit each morning to see if I'm needed there."

Icily, Catherine asked, "Did you see Georgy on your way here? I must speak with her."

"I heard her playing with Charley and Walter in their room."

Silently, his wife left the kitchen.

Over dinner and afterwards Dickens regaled Catherine and Georgy with news of his London trip, especially what he considered the great triumph of his reading *The Chimes* at Forster's house. Around ten o'clock the family retired.

Hours later, a timid, candle-bearing servant in nightclothes shook Dickens' shoulder. He opened his eyes.

"Sir, a note from Brignole Rosso has come. It seems there is a crisis of some sort."

Dickens put his fingers to his lips and gently rose from bed. His wife slept on. He followed the servant out of the room and took the note from him.

> *Charles,*
>> *I pray your request to be called at any time was genuine. Madame is in a terrible condition. I am at a loss what to do.*
>>> *If at all possible, please come to her.*
>>>> *Emile.*

Sleep fell away from Dickens like a loosened cloak. He grew alert, eagerly craving the opportunity to put his powers to the test. He took the candle from the servant, waved him away, and reentered the bedroom to dress.

Midway through dressing he heard his wife's voice. "What in heaven's name are you doing? Is there a fire?"

"No, no, Kate. Go on back to sleep. Madame de la Rue is ill. Very ill. Emile thinks I can be of some use. He has sent a note."

"To you? Now? What time is it?"

"Just after three."

"Who do they think...?"

Dickens interrupted, "I'll be home when I can. Go back to sleep." He strode to the door and left the room.

Emile de la Rue, clad in nightclothes and a robe, awaited him when he reached the Brignole Rosse. The rooms were candle-lit and eerie.

"I cannot thank you enough, Charles."

"Where is Madame?"

"In the bedroom. Come."

De la Rue preceded Dickens, carrying a silver holder with three candles. When Dickens entered the room and the dim light fell on Augusta de la Rue, he felt as if he had been slammed in the chest again by the invisible pole across the road.

Madame de la Rue lay on the floor rolled into a tight ball, her knees drawn up to her stomach. Her head, which Dickens could not even identify from where he stood, hunched somewhere down on her chest, and her arms wrapped tightly around her body. Through Dickens' mind flitted the thought that somehow the woman had melted and congealed into the shapeless, hardened mass before him.

"She has been like this for nearly an hour," said de la Rue.

"No, no. Leave me be," the woman muttered. A flow of indistinguishable moans followed. Then silence.

"Leave us, Emile. I will see what I can do."

Hesitantly, de la Rue left. When Dickens heard the click of the door, he approached the huddled woman. He placed the candles de la Rue had left on the side table and knelt next to Augusta.

Her long hair spread over her as if she were trying to hide under it. Dickens brushed it aside and followed it to its source to locate where Augusta had buried her head. The woman so contorted herself only her right cheek was visible.

"Augusta," he called softly. He stroked her cheek with the back of the second and third fingers of his right hand. "Augusta, it is Charles. I've come to help you."

Augusta moaned. "He's come back," the woman whispered and moaned again.

"I will rid you of him." Dickens knew he had to find some way to get Augusta to face him and open her eyes so *his* eyes could do their work. He continued to stroke her cheek and talk to her. "You had a very good day after I left, Augusta, and I will give you many more good days. Day after day you will grow stronger. Together we will fight the phantom who is attacking you."

A tremor passed through Augusta's body, and her head quivered.

"Do not fear the phantom, Augusta. I am here. I am with you." On and on he spoke, gently stroking Augusta's cheek. Ever so slowly Dickens felt the tension in her body abate.

"Can you stretch out your right arm, Augusta? Stretch out your arm for me."

Dickens repeated his demand slowly and firmly, all the while stroking the woman's cheek. For a moment the fingers on Augusta's right hand quivered and then her arm moved. Dickens could now see her face. He lay down on his stomach, his face only inches from the woman's face.

"Open your eyes, Augusta. I am here. You will see that I am here. It is Charles." If only he could get her eyes open, Dickens knew his visual ray would do its work.

He filled Augusta's mind with repetition after repetition of his demand.

"Open your eyes. Open your eyes. Open your eyes."

At last her eyelids fluttered and opened. Dickens

talked on, ordering her to move her left arm. Her legs. Her head.

Finally, Dickens heard words indicating to him he had taken command of the woman's malady. She looked into his eyes and responded. "Oh, Charles. Thank God."

"Sit up, Augusta. Can you?"

With Dickens' help the woman sat up and leaned back against the bed.

Through the dancing shadows in the flickering candle-lit room, Augusta stared intently into Dickens' eyes as shadow and light played across his face.

"I am going to make you sleep, Augusta. The same safe and restful sleep I gave you this morning. I'm going to burden your eyes again with those same heavy weights I placed on them this morning. You will have no choice but to sleep. You will enter a private place where only you can go." With his index fingers Dickens gently stroked Augusta's temples and continued to talk to her.

"Rise, Augusta. You must return to your bed."

Dickens helped her to her feet and gently saw her into bed. He covered her with the counterpane and pulled a chair next to her. On and on he spoke, not touching her now but passing his hand back and forth rhythmically before her fluttering eyelids.

Where moments before he desperately needed Augusta's eyes to open, he now desperately wanted to see them close; close into the same peaceful sleep he had induced in her that morning.

With a muttered, "Charles," Augusta's eyelids finally fell shut. Dickens stopped his gestures and let her sleep.

After ten minutes he rose, took the candles, and left the room.

Emile de la Rue sprang from a sofa in the dark main *sala*.

"Sit, Emile. She is back in bed and resting."

"Thank you, Charles. I don't know what else to say to you."

"I will come back in the morning, with your permission."

"Of course you may come. You do not require any permission. You are needed here, Charles."

Dickens nodded his agreement.

"I believe she will rest through the night. I don't think anything else need be done for now."

De la Rue extended his hand. Dickens took it, understanding the inexpressible gratitude de la Rue offered him.

As they walked toward the apartment door, de la Rue said, more to himself than to his companion, "Why is this happening to her?"

The phantom, Dickens thought. The phantom—still Augusta's secret, still unknown to her husband. Dickens knew he could not break Augusta's confidence.

"We will deal with it," he responded.

He left the Brignole Rosso and returned home.

Chapter Seven

Each morning for the next ten mornings Dickens visited the Brignole Rosso punctually at ten o'clock. (Dickens new daily schedule did not thrill his wife, who was particularly put out by a Christmas day visit.) Each morning he placed Augusta de la Rue, eager for his visits and his treatments, into a mesmeric trance to induce the rest she found impossible to get at night. Dreams came—dreams where Augusta's phantom prowled—but not dreams which had the fearsome consequences of the night that left her hunched up on the bedroom floor moaning.

Friday, January 3. Emile de la Rue had left for Turin, where his firm had an office. Before he left he petitioned Dickens to keep a close eye on his wife. Dickens readily complied, intent on learning more about Augusta's phantom.

Dickens found Madame de la Rue in the sitting room dressed for the day when he arrived punctually at ten. She rose, smiled, and stretched out a hand to him.

"Charles."

"How are you feeling today, Augusta?"

"I rested well last night." Her left eye fluttered, and a moment later her left cheek quivered.

"Let's sit." Dickens scanned the room for servants and saw they were alone. "I told you that worse might precede better. Nights like the one before Christmas may recur."

"Yes, but that hasn't happened."

"It may. If it does, it will not be a setback. Augusta, if we want to permanently cure you of your affliction, we must deal with the phantom haunting your dreams."

Augusta deliberately moved her head erect.

"The dreams have weakened," she said softly, as if wishing to avoid what she knew Dickens had in mind.

Dickens shook his head. "No, we must deal with it."

Augusta lacked the power to argue with Dickens.

"How?" she whispered.

Dickens had given great thought to the information Augusta had shared with him. The questions he wanted answered were listed in his mind.

"Why haven't you told Emile of your dreams?"

Augusta could not face Dickens. She looked down at her lap. She quickly put her left hand to her cheek, which began to throb and shook her head.

"I don't know."

"Look at me, Augusta. Remember what I told you—about there being a state between waking and sleep—a state where more thoughts can fill your mind than can be remembered in weeks of dreaming?"

Augusta nodded.

"We will go there. I am going to attach those weights, those terribly heavy weights to your eyelids, Augusta." It had become increasingly easy for Dickens to induce a trance in Augusta—something Dickens now depended on. He reached out, took the woman's left hand, and stroked the back of it.

"Look into my eyes and don't look away. I am going

to take you to a safe place; a place where no harm can befall you; a place from which you will be able to speak to me with truth and in confidence. Look at me. Look at me. Don't turn away." On Dickens spoke as he stared into the woman's eyes with all the power he could muster and stroked her hand. At the first flutter of her eyelids, Dickens ceased stroking her hand, held it only, and with his other hand made gentle passes before Augusta's face as he talked about the safe place and about protecting her.

As he repeated his words, his mind wandered to his plan. Augusta refused to mention her dreams to her husband. Her condition had arisen shortly after their marriage. Quite possibly her new marriage and her new husband were the source of the phantom and the cause of her malady. He needed to eliminate this possibility before moving on to other theories.

"Augusta, how did you meet Emile?"

Dickens kept a hold on Augusta's hand. Her eyes were closed and she breathed in the steady rhythm Dickens recognized from previous trances. She responded, "I love Emile. I love him. I was in Turin. With my father, a missionary. We were on our way here to Genoa, visiting sites. We met Emile at a gathering, a church gathering. Emile was about to leave for Egypt on banking business. We got on well but he had to leave on his trip."

Nothing more came. Dickens waited a brief time then asked, "Did you remain in Turin while Emile was away?"

"We moved on to Rome."

"Did anything happen in Rome? Anything you associate with Emile?"

"I met Rodney."

Dickens stared in astonishment as a tear formed in Augusta's right eye and trickled down her cheek.

"Can you tell me about Rodney?"

Augusta's left cheek began violent convulsions and her breathing quickened. Frightened, Dickens stroked her hand and reassured her again. When her cheek relaxed and her breathing settled, he gently woke her by repeating her name with a command to return to him.

When she opened her eyes, he dropped her hand and asked, "How do you feel?"

The woman drew in a deep breath. "I feel fine. What...did you...I can't recall anything."

"That is as it should be, Augusta." Though Dickens managed to keep his tone of voice gentle, his mind raced. Rodney? Who the devil was Rodney? The name had never come up before. Should he chance interrogating Augusta openly about the name? Elliotson had cautioned him against confronting a patient with information newly learned under trance unless the patient herself raised the subject afterwards. Impatience to know burned inside of Dickens, but as impatient as he felt, his discipline held fast and he refrained from further questions.

"You will have a good day, Augusta. You should get out for a while," he urged, smiling.

"I certainly will try." She returned his smile. "I do feel good today."

Dickens rose. "I will be at home. You know you can summon me anytime. Don't hesitate. Promise me."

Augusta looked down. "You've proven that. I

promise."

After a few moments of idle chatter, Dickens went home.

Throughout the day the name Rodney filled his mind. The lack of facts, though, to whirl around his mind and sort into some sensible explanation had Dickens yearning for his next morning's visit. He kept himself occupied with his children and the preparations for the Twelfth Night celebrations—magic shows, pantomimes, charades and small theatrical performances—still to come. After breakfast next day and a long walk through the city, he made his call on Augusta de la Rue.

Augusta was dressed and waiting for him.

Dickens greeted her and asked how she had slept.

She looked away then back at Dickens. "These dreams." She began to weep.

Augusta sat on the sofa and Dickens moved next to her. He reached for her hand. At his touch she threw her head back and breathed deeply.

"What is wrong with me?" With her free hand she rubbed at her eyes.

"Can you tell me what was in your dreams?"

"Only that...*he*...was in them."

"He?"

"That figure. Oh, Charles, it's all a mixed up fog of images."

"We made some progress yesterday, Augusta."

She turned quickly. "I don't remember..."

Dickens rose, pulled over a chair, and sat opposite her.

"Are you willing to continue?"

"Oh, yes, Charles. Yes."

"Then relax. Breathe deeply and relax." Dickens began to stroke her hand and leaned nearer. "Don't look away from my eyes." It had taken no more than three minutes to bring the woman into trance the day before. Today it took perhaps four.

"We are going to the same safe place we visited yesterday, Augusta," Dickens intoned.

Augusta lowered her head slightly.

"Who is Rodney?"

Dickens watched carefully as Augusta's breathing rate sped up. He stroked her hand, reassured her, calmed her. He repeated the question. Elliotson had told him repeating one question over and over would often take away the shock of having heard the question in the first place and could bring the patient into a relaxed state and invite a response.

Dickens asked again, "Who is Rodney?"

Suddenly, Augusta's eyes snapped open and startled Dickens. She clasped his hand tightly as fear etched her features. "Where is my brother?" she cried. "Where is Charles?"

Charles? First Rodney, now Charles?

"Who is Charles?" Dickens asked calmly.

"Where is my brother? Charles is gone."

"I am right here, Augusta."

"No, no. Charles. Where is my brother?"

Augusta's eyes closed and Dickens looked on, his stomach balled into a tense knot, as the woman's breathing settled into the rhythmic breathing of trance.

74

Dickens admitted to himself he had no idea where to go. Lamely, he repeated, "Who is Rodney?"

But Augusta de la Rue remained quiet. Dickens allowed her to rest in trance for another few minutes as he tried to come up with a new approach, another question, anything. He finally surrendered to the realization he needed more information. Who were these people she mentioned? Did they...had they...actually existed, or were they merely guises of the woman's phantom making an appearance for Dickens? Gently and slowly he woke her.

She dropped his hand and put her two hands to her temples.

"What is it?" Dickens asked.

"I felt a headache...but no. I'll be fine."

Dickens hated to leave her but he rose nonetheless. Not knowing maddened him. "I will be back this afternoon, Augusta. With your consent, of course."

"Do you need to ask? But why?" Her face turned serious. Dickens' expression indicated it would not be a social call.

"We are making progress," Dickens explained with all the certitude he could muster and they parted.

Angus Fletcher lived on the edge of Genoa in inexpensive rooms atop a warehouse. The living conditions were Spartan, but a multitude of windows faced south. The situation proved conducive both to his pocketbook and his sculpting. Dickens set out for Fletcher's directly after leaving Augusta.

Fletcher opened his door, tools of the trade in his

hands. "Charles, what a surprise. Come in. Come in."

Dickens looked over the space. Fletcher lived in one large room crowded with statuary both complete and in progress. A light pale dust covered the floor. Various hammers and chisels were arrayed on a long table against the far wall. The view from the windows consisted of the few buildings further out on the edge of town than Fletcher's and a tiny corner of the harbor, a small splash of blue amid a tangle of grays and browns. Dickens spotted a bed in a corner. On a shelf over the bed he saw a small bust of himself, one of Fletcher's practice busts.

Fletcher removed his apron and tossed it on the long table along with the tools he carried.

"I didn't know you would be working on a Saturday, Angus."

"I was about to stop for some wine and cheese. You'll join me, of course."

"Thank you, I will." He removed his hat and coat and looked for a place—a clean place—to lay them. Finally, he tossed them onto a chair which had for the most part escaped the dusty ravages of Fletcher's workday.

Carrying a bottle of wine, some cheese, plates, and a knife, Fletcher led Dickens to a small round table and two chairs in a corner near a window. Fletcher set the food and wine on the table.

"I haven't seen you since your trip," said Fletcher, pouring the wine. Dickens, always happy to report on his reading of *The Chimes,* rushed through his travelogue to get to it. "Maclise sketched the scene. Carlyle was very impressed and I had Macready, the great actor, in tears,"

Dickens laughed. "I've already received a note from Forster telling me how well *The Chimes* is selling. He'll write again in mid-January, but the book seems quite the success."

"Congratulations," said Fletcher, wiping his fingers on his dusty black pants.

"Angus, I've come today for a special reason."

Fletcher refilled Dickens' glass. Dickens paused and watched the golden waterfall of wine from the bottle.

"How much do you know about Madame De la Rue?"

Fletcher sipped his wine before cutting a piece of cheese and popping it into his mouth. He shook his head dismissively as he chewed.

"What is it you want to know?"

"Do you know a Rodney or a Charles associated with her? Does she have a brother?"

Fletcher nodded knowingly and helped himself to more cheese.

"Was it she who told you about it or Emile?"

"No, Emile is away in Turin. I am asking you this in confidence, Angus. If you're not comfortable telling me anything *entre nous* then tell me nothing at all, but whatever you tell me must remain between us." Dickens knew he could not let Emile know of his prowling about in Augusta's mind. Since Augusta had kept her dreams of the phantom a secret from Emile, he would leave it to Augusta to decide what to disclose to him.

"It's not a secret. It's not a topic of much conversation in Genoa either but it's no secret."

"Go on."

"I don't profess to know the whole story, but I've

heard mention of it."

"Go on, Angus," Dickens sighed. Dickens wondered where patient people got their patience.

"Well, Madame de la Rue met Emile on some trip she took with her father."

"Her father was a missionary?"

"Yes. Emile had to go off on business and, to hear him tell it, he had already fallen in love with her. She met a young man name of Dowd. Rodney Dowd. A young fellow, an engineer of some kind as I remember. In Rome, I believe. Planned to marry him, according to what I hear. Rejected de la Rue. The Charles you mention was her brother. Older by a couple of years—maybe twenty, twenty-one. Seems he and this Dowd had an argument. Patched it up. Went off on a hike together but only one of them returned. The brother, Charles. He claimed he and Dowd got separated and he never saw him again. No one ever found the body. Lots of gorges, crevices, where they'd hiked."

Dickens began to see where a phantom might easily spring from this tale.

"Go on, Angus. Was it murder?"

"Couldn't be proved. Oddly enough de la Rue had returned to Rome by then on business and was visiting her family. He claimed to have heard a loud argument between the two men the night before their trek. There was no corroboration of that, however. The brother Charles stood in disgrace, though nothing could be proved against him. Ended up going to Australia, as I recall."

"Did Emile ever say what the two men argued about?"

"He told everyone they argued over whether the lady

should marry Dowd or not."

"And did her brother's account agree?"

"No, he claimed the argument never happened, of course. Proclaimed his innocence but his reputation was in tatters. Went to Australia, as I said."

"And then?"

"And then what?"

"How did Madame de la Rue end up marrying Emile?"

Fletcher shrugged. "He asked and she eventually accepted. That's all I know."

Dickens sat back—he had been leaning eagerly forward—and sipped from his wineglass.

"Angus, I'd rather not have Emile know I asked about any of this."

"Yes, Charles, I heard you the first time. It's between us."

Dickens bobbed his head once and absent-mindedly cut off four cubes of cheese as the conversation moved onto more pedestrian topics. Thirty minutes later, Dickens bid Fletcher farewell.

Dickens walked back toward the Peschiere deep in thought. Augusta's phantom could easily be the Dowd boy, her lost lover; or Charles, her exiled brother; or a combination of the two, merging to forge a symbol of the whole episode, an episode no doubt very painful for her. He would have to get Augusta to acknowledge the source of the phantom. Elliotson assured him that getting a patient to realize the source of the distress and confront it, discuss it, and eventually master it, offered a certain pathway to cure.

Eager as he was to put his plan into effect, Dickens decided it would be best to spend a few hours at home—he did not want to face Catherine's reaction to his staying out all day and, in her mind, spending it with Madame de la Rue. Catherine lately exhibited increasing signs of jealousy. Misplaced, unnecessary, and offensive, to be sure, but that was Catherine. It would not be the first time her insecurity had raised its ugly head. Her reaction to his day notwithstanding, he would return to the Brignole Rosso before dinner and place Augusta under trance. This time, however, he knew what questions to ask.

Chapter Eight

As Dickens approached the entrance to the Peschiere, he heard his name called. He turned and recognized Giovanni, a servant from the Brignole Rosso.

In rapid Italian, Giovanni said, "Madame has sent me for you, Monsieur Dickens. She says she is ill and needs you."

"What's wrong?"

Giovanni touched his head. "Headache. She is in bed."

"Have you been to my house for me?"

Giovanni said he had not.

Dickens paused. His wife would have to wait. He followed Giovanni toward the Brignole Rosso.

Dickens entered Augusta de la Rue's bedroom, leaving the door ajar as a concession to propriety. He pulled a chair to her bedside.

"Augusta. It's Charles. I'm here."

Augusta lay still, her eyes closed, but at the sound of Dickens' voice her eyes sprang open.

"Charles!" She stared confusedly at him a moment. "Oh, my head, Charles. Not long after you left...it's been throbbing horribly."

Dickens took Augusta's hand and spoke to her, concentrating on his tone of voice.

"Don't let this frighten you. I told you your condition could easily worsen on the way to a cure. This is what is happening. I *will* cure you." Dickens scolded himself for altering his tone and emphasizing 'will.' Reassured and reassuring. Focus. Stay calm. "I will take your headache away. You know what to do, Augusta. Look into my eyes and don't turn away."

This time it took more than five minutes for the woman's eyelids to flutter closed and Dickens to note her steady, even, peaceful respiration. He let her rest for ten minutes more and then began.

"I want to speak with you, Augusta. You know where we are going. We are going to the safe place where nothing can harm you. Will you go with me there?"

Dickens felt his stomach shrink into a nervous mass as he waited to see whether Augusta would speak or simply sleep on. She inclined her head in acquiescence.

Dickens sighed in relief and composed himself.

"I know where your brother, Charles, is."

Augusta's eyes opened slightly.

"He is safe and happy. He cannot be hurt."

A faint smile visited and fled from the woman's lips.

"I know where Rodney is. He also is safe and cannot be hurt."

Augusta moved her head as if trying to settle deeper into the pillow.

"Which of these two men is the phantom who visits your dreams?"

The woman began breathing more rapidly. Dickens felt the pressure of her hand on his strengthen. Her left cheek twitched.

Dickens soothed her and moved off the topic,

reassuring her of her safety. It took five minutes before he managed to return her to quiet trance.

"Tell me about Rodney," Dickens said quietly. He waited a moment and then repeated the question, watching carefully for some physiological reaction from the woman. He repeated the question twice more. Augusta's eyes fluttered and opened slightly.

"I met Rodney in Rome. He visited me often. We walked out together often."

"Did you love him?"

"I love my husband," she responded, a tinge of alarm in her voice.

"Of course you do. I know that. But you met Rodney before you married your husband. Did you love Rodney?"

Dickens repeated the question until the woman answered, "I loved Rodney."

"Did he ask you to marry him?"

She answered right away. "He planned to ask me."

"How do you know?"

"Charles told me. Charles. Oh, Charles." Suddenly, her eyes sprang wide open. "Where is my brother? Where is my brother?"

Dickens decided he had put the woman through enough and worked quickly to quiet her. With his free hand he made passes before her open eyes and around her head. Her facial spasms lessened. Her cheek and mouth, however, continued to quiver. He spoke to her quietly and eventually her eyes fluttered closed. Dickens watched over her for another twenty minutes and then quietly went home.

Catherine's greeting tried his patience. "Have you

been with that woman all day?"

"No, I had lunch with Angus. I walked over to his studio."

Catherine sniffed loudly. "The children have been asking for you."

"Then I will go to them." He walked off.

On his way to the Brignole Rosso next morning, Dickens realized he would have to hurry his treatment of Madame de la Rue along. His family's previously planned months-long tour of Italy began on January 19th. This gave him barely two weeks.

The session that day and for the next few days produced little in the way of new information. There were even two days when Madame de la Rue felt a treatment unnecessary. Dickens urged her to a treatment anyway, fearing his power over her would diminish with missed treatments. Those two days, however, she insisted and he had to accept the rejection.

Emile de la Rue returned to the Brignole Rosso on Friday, January 10. Dickens informed him he had been helping his wife rest each day. There had been headaches, he reported, but he had been able to alleviate them in minutes. His wife's nights had been restless but there had been no severe attacks like the one which left her crumpled on the floor. De la Rue found it encouraging when he heard of his wife's two normal, untreated days. He thanked Dickens and begged him to keep on with his treatments, a petition heartily seconded by Augusta.

Dickens continued to visit the Brignole Rosso daily. On Monday, January 13, however, Augusta had an attack which shattered the quiet of an evening at the Peschiere. A little past eight in the evening with dinner long over, Dickens sat in his office off the grand *sala* going over correspondence. He could hear his children playing and Georgy's voice in the distance. Catherine's voice, shrill and insistent cut through the evening. Something, he knew, was wrong. He left his office and walked across the *sala* toward the staircase in the direction of Catherine's voice. At the bottom of the stairs, his wife engaged in an animated discussion with Anne, her maid. Dickens started down the stairs. Catherine heard him and looked up.

"That woman—that woman has sent for you again?" she asked through clenched teeth.

Dickens noticed Giovanni standing by the front door.

"What has happened?" Dickens asked.

"You'll have to ask him," his wife answered.

Dickens approached the servant.

"Monsieur Dickens, it is Madame. You must come. She is...she is shaking and moaning."

"I will come immediately," Dickens responded in Italian.

"You're going to her?" Catherine asked in disbelief. Dickens could see how she restrained herself in front of Anne and Giovanni.

"Madame de la Rue is ill. You know I'm committed to helping her. You were there when I made the commitment. I will be back as soon as possible."

Dickens went upstairs and changed his slippers for shoes, spent a moment arranging his hair, found his great coat, and left the house.

Emile de la Rue met Dickens at the door and led him to the bedroom where Augusta lay under the counterpane. The muscles of her face danced uncontrollably.

"She has been like this for over an hour," de la Rue reported.

Dickens looked at him and de la Rue understood. "I will be outside in the sitting room." Dickens waited until de la Rue closed the door behind him and began his usual procedures. He pulled a chair over, took the woman's hand, and stroked it. He spoke to her. For the first few minutes the woman simply moaned, "My head; my head," but Dickens would not be stopped. He continued his usual patter about her being safe and his being there to cure her. Alternately, he stroked the back of her hand and made slow passes with both hands around her face and head. Fifteen, then twenty minutes passed. Slowly her facial contortions abated. After thirty minutes the muscles in her face quieted.

"Augusta, I've taken you to the safe place. We are there now. Together. Both of us. Can you hear me?"

Dickens patiently repeated the question until Augusta bent her head in response.

"Has the phantom come to you tonight, Augusta?"

"Yes. Oh, yes."

Augusta's hand clutched his tightly.

"What did the phantom look like?"

"Bloody. The phantom wore a bloody mask. He would not let me see his face."

Bloody? "What did the phantom do?" The woman's voice remained calm at the mention of the phantom, surprising Dickens. He felt doubly surprised when she

86

answered question after question.

"He took me to a field."

"What did he do in the field?"

"He pointed."

"What did he point at?"

"Low mountains. Hills. A waterfall."

"Do you know where these hills and waterfall are?"

"Rome. Rome. I walked there with him. I..." Dickens saw Augusta's mouth quiver and he feared losing her.

"Who did you walk there with? Who took you there?" Dickens knew immediately he had erred. His voice had risen in desperation, and he had asked two questions at once, a thing Elliotson specifically warned him against. He tried to recoup.

"Who did you walk there with when you were in Rome?" Dickens felt a strong urge to add, "Your brother? Rodney?" But he held his piece.

"Where is my brother?" the woman whispered. The muscles in her left cheek began to dance, and Dickens spoke to her and calmed her. When she returned to a quiet state, he considered. She was communicative tonight. He would try once more.

"Who did you walk with in the field in Rome?"

Four repetitions of the question brought no response.

There were only five days until he left on his tour of Italy. He must press on. If she would not answer that question he would try another.

"You said Rodney planned to ask you to marry him. Who told you so?"

She answered without delay. "Charles. He and Rodney were friends."

Friends? Angus told him they quarreled.

"When was Rodney going to ask you to become his wife?"

As soon as she heard the question, the left corner of the woman's mouth began to dance.

Quickly, Dickens urged to himself.

"When was Rodney going to ask you to become his wife?"

"That day. That day. Oh, where is my brother? Where?"

Tension filled Augusta de la Rue's face. Dickens calmed her and led her back into quiet trance. He let her remain there, unwilling to put her through any more that night. He accepted Emile de la Rue's thanks and left. He would pick up the story from there tomorrow. He would have the story out of Augusta de la Rue even if he had to move into the Brignole Rosso and mesmerize the woman five times a day. He would have the story out of her, and he would have it before he left Genoa.

Dickens returned home to a quiet house just before eleven. As he lay in bed next to a sleeping Catherine, he counted backwards. They were leaving the Peschiere on Sunday. He realized his getting away from home on Saturday, what with packing and organizing, getting correspondence in order, would be next to impossible. The de la Rues were giving a farewell dinner for him on Friday evening. Dickens knew Catherine did not want to go but also knew that she would go. He had told her so as a certainty. It gave him only four days. He closed his eyes but sleep had no chance to establish its dominion over him, and he lay staring into darkness, dissecting the bits of the story he had extracted from Augusta de la Rue. A bloody phantom. An incipient engagement. Dickens knew he did not have enough information to complete the picture, though. He felt as if one of his twenty-number serials lacked parts nine through sixteen.

On Tuesday, Wednesday, and Thursday Dickens appeared at the Brignole Rosso by ten o'clock. Maddeningly, Augusta de la Rue merely repeated things she had already revealed to Dickens. Her nightly headaches continued but not of a severity requiring Dickens midnight presence. The phantom did not reappear. Until Friday.

Chapter Nine

Dickens had always delayed his visits to the Brignole Rosso until ten in the morning—in his mind, the earliest well-mannered hour possible. But Friday morning, January 17, Dickens received a note from Emile de la Rue at seven-forty-five as he sat at his breakfast table. Madame felt ill and would he please come quickly.

When he arrived, Augusta de la Rue lay in bed moaning, her eyes closed, breathing at a rapid rate. Spasms rippled through her body, though for once her facial muscles were still. With no hesitation de la Rue closed the bedroom door on Dickens and his wife.

Dickens began his work and in fifteen minutes Augusta's breathing calmed and she lay still.

"Do you remember what you were telling me, Augusta?" asked Dickens, determined to drive the story forward on this, his final opportunity.

It took three repetitions of the question, but finally the woman nodded.

"Do you remember you told me about Rodney planning to ask to marry you?"

She nodded again.

Even though he felt certain the phantom bound the disease to the woman and the woman to the disease, he would not mention the phantom until last. Perhaps then she would remain in quiet trance and answer his other questions.

Before Dickens could even posit a question, though,

the woman spoke.

"Charles told me Rodney would ask me to be his wife and give me a ring after they returned from the hike. Charles said Rodney had things he wanted to discuss with him. Charles told me he had seen the beautiful ring Rodney had for me. He said the ring once belonged to Rodney's mother. Diamonds and rubies set in gold. It was so beautiful. How it shone!"

This puzzled Dickens. She spoke as if she had actually seen the ring.

"Did Charles tell you how the ring shone?"

"No."

Dickens paused. Augusta's left hand clenched into a fist. He opened it gently and held it.

"How do you know the ring shone so?"

"I saw it."

"You saw the ring?"

"Yes?"

"When did you see the ring?"

Dickens grimaced as Augusta clamped her hand around his.

"That night."

"The night of the...accident?"

The woman nodded once.

Rodney was dead by then, his body lost. How could she have seen the ring? Perhaps her brother had brought it back with him? No, that didn't make sense. It would have made him even more a suspect than he had been.

"Where did you see the ring?"

No answer.

"Where did you see the ring?"

The woman's breathing quickened.

"Where did you see the ring?" Dickens desperately wanted this one more answer out of her but knew he could lose the woman by overly upsetting her. He tried to keep his voice calm. "Where did you see the ring?"

"Don't tell anyone he had it."

"I will not. Who had the ring, Augusta?"

"Please, don't tell anyone he hid it. I saw it. He didn't know. Don't tell. Promise me. Please, don't tell."

"I promise you I will never reveal what you tell me, Augusta. Who had the ring?"

Augusta de la Rue whispered, "The phantom had the ring." She straight away broke down, moaning, shaking, and clasping Dickens' hand so tightly Dickens could not release himself from her grasp.

It took Dickens fifteen minutes to settle the woman back into quiet trance. He dared probe no further what with de la Rue waiting for him in the room outside. After ten quiet minutes he joined de la Rue and declared the session a success. "Your wife is sleeping quietly," Dickens reported.

"Charles, you have been a godsend," de la Rue gushed. He walked to the bedroom door and looked inside. He closed the door quietly and returned to Dickens. "I hope she will be well enough tonight for your party."

Dickens thought quickly. "Emile, I have an idea. With your permission Kate and I will arrive early, say six o'clock. I will mesmerize Madame once again, and while she is in trance I will pave the way for a quiet night for her."

"By all means. Have you breakfasted? Let me feed

you at least for all the trouble you've taken already today."

Dickens laughed. "No, no. I've eaten." Catherine loomed on his mind. He did not want to stay any longer than necessary. He would be on the road with her for three months, and they needed to be on the best possible terms. "But about my trip."

A look of worry crossed de la Rue's face

"We must keep in touch while I'm away." This afternoon he would attempt to bar the phantom from Augusta's dreams. He believed himself powerful enough to exile the phantom, at least for a time. He could not be certain, though, for how long. While he was away, the phantom could easily return and reassert his ascendancy over Augusta...and over him.

"Is there anything I can do? There must be something."

"Will you keep a journal while I'm gone?"

De la Rue looked perplexed. "And in the journal...?"

"Daily reports on Madame's health. How she sleeps, the nature of any attacks. I am prepared to return to Genoa if need be. And, of course, I will be back come April."

"No, no. I could not ask you to break off your tour. If only I could do what you can do."

"There is no time to teach you the skills of a mesmerist, Emile. I want you to write me. Tonight I will bring you an itinerary of my trip. Believe what I say, Emile, my travels will be solely guided by your letters. Think, also, of joining us, perhaps in Rome. We will be there in a few weeks and then again for Holy Week in March."

"Perhaps in March. In two weeks is impossible."

"Consider it. Also, I am going to tell your wife tonight that every morning at ten and every evening at eleven, I will think of her and try to induce trance from wherever I am. I promise to be faithful in this. I will ask her to concentrate and be receptive to me, and I want you to note her behavior in your journal at those times. Write me—daily if need be but certainly weekly even if only to tell me that, blessedly, there is only good news to report."

"Is it possible? To be in contact at such a distance?"

"It has been done by others." Elliotson had mentioned this long-distance phenomenon in passing during their conversation in London, not as something Dickens could rely on but merely as an example of the power of mesmerism. Dickens assumed what one mesmerist could do, he could do.

De la Rue shook his head in amazement. "I will do whatever you say, Charles. You may depend on it."

As Dickens expected, Catherine gave a chill acceptance to his demanding she be ready to go to the de la Rues early.

The de la Rues greeted Dickens and his wife with heartfelt gratitude and praise for the time Dickens had sacrificed to treat Madame de la Rue and the positive results of the treatment. Emile de la Rue led Catherine aside to continue reporting on the mesmeric prowess of her husband, and Catherine had little choice but to follow him. When they were out of sight, Dickens and Augusta de la Rue retreated into the bedroom. They sat in chairs and faced each other.

"Charles, you have my eternal gratitude for what you've done for me."

Dickens brushed aside her thanks, knowing that until the phantom left her dreams, she had little hope of a permanent cure.

Augusta smiled slightly. "I haven't told you of my dreams."

Concern flashed across Dickens' face.

"No, no. Good dreams. Peaceful dreams."

"What do you mean?"

Augusta drew a deep sigh. She looked down shyly then with a quiet, trusting voice asked, "Did you know I was nearly engaged once? I don't mean to Emile."

Tension rippled through Dickens. He squared his shoulders to relax and said, "Oh? Tell me about it."

"You hadn't heard?"

"Angus mentioned something to me."

"Ah. You do know then about the accident."

"Angus mentioned it."

Augusta nodded resignedly as if acknowledging that the past could not be hidden. "I've been dreaming of my brother and Rodney. My brother's name is Charles, you know?"

"Yes, go on."

"There is not much more to tell. They've been pleasant dreams of Charles and Rodney. I miss them both very much," she added quietly.

"Hadn't you dreamed of them before now?"

Augusta shook her head slowly. "Not in any way I remember. Certainly not with this wonderful warmth."

"You say nearly engaged."

"The accident occurred on the day Rodney was going

to propose. At least so my brother told me. Rodney had even chosen the ring."

Dickens kept a tight rein on himself and with as unemotional a voice as he could manage he asked, "Did you ever see the ring?"

"See it?" Augusta smiled and shook her head. "No." Suddenly, a tic began to quiver in her left cheek.

Dickens studied her intently. "Did your brother see the ring?"

"Oh, yes. He said it was very beautiful. A gold ring with diamonds and rubies."

"What happened to the ring?"

Dickens saw Augusta's expression sink into sadness.

"Lost with Rodney."

"You never saw it then?"

Augusta offered a look of befuddlement. "No. How could I? People suspected my brother but could prove nothing against him. Yet how could he prove he had nothing to do with Rodney's disappearance. It was impossible." Her left cheek began pulsing. "Emile treated me very kindly during that time. We...we eventually..." She did not finish.

Dickens knew he had better move on. "We don't have much time, Augusta. I want to put you into trance. I am going to banish the phantom from your dreams. Listen carefully to me." He explained to her, as he had explained to her husband, how he would attempt to be in touch with her while away. She nodded and asked no questions.

Dickens began to make passes with his hands and speak to her and in only three minutes Augusta passed into trance. He had not planned what he was about to do but he felt it worth the try.

"Augusta, tell me again about the ring Rodney planned to give you."

She answered immediately. "Oh, a beautiful ring. Gold, diamonds and rubies."

"Did you ever see this ring with your own eyes?"

No answer.

The question repeated.

No answer.

Repeated.

No answer. The pace of Augusta's respiration increased.

"Did you ever see this ring with your own eyes?"

"Yes."

"When?"

A long pause.

"When?"

"The night of the accident." Then in a quieter voice, "Where is my brother?"

"Where did you see the ring?"

Augusta's eye fluttered open, and she looked at Dickens, who felt a terrible chill sweep over him.

"Where did you see the ring?"

"In his room."

"Whose room?"

"The phantom's room. In the phantom's room. Masked. Bloody. The phantom." At each utterance the woman's eyes opened a bit wider.

Dickens quieted the woman as what she told him raced through his thoughts. In trance she professed to have seen the ring. Conscious, she denied it. Dickens put his confidence in the truth emerging during trance. She'd seen the ring in the phantom's room. It could only be her brother's room. If she had seen the ring in her brother's room on the night of the so-called accident, she could easily believe her brother did away with Rodney for some unknown reason. Perhaps the ring, which sounded quite valuable, was the reason. She could only face the realization that her brother killer her lover in dreams or in trance when her brother appeared to her in the guise of a phantom, masked and bloody.

"I am banishing the phantom from your dreams, Augusta. I forbid you to allow him to come to you. The phantom is gone and he will never return to haunt you again." On and on Dickens went, banishing the phantom as powerfully as his command of language permitted. Augusta's eyes drooped closed and stayed closed until Dickens finished. Slowly and carefully, he woke her.

She blinked as if looking into a strong light until she found Dickens' eyes and relaxed.

"How do you feel?" Dickens asked, forcing a smile.

"Fine. I feel fine." She rose.

"Augusta, beginning tomorrow and continuing every day thereafter, find a quiet place at the times I told you and open your mind to me. We will defeat this phantom. Defeat it utterly."

Augusta put her hand on Dickens' arm a moment, and Dickens led her back into the sitting room.

Chapter Ten

Sunday January 19, 1845. Dickens and his wife set out on their tour of southern Italy in the capable hands of Louis Roche, their inestimable courier. They visited Rome during Carnival Week before moving on to Naples, and everywhere they went Dickens stayed on the lookout for letters from Emile de la Rue. Through the rest of January and into February letters found him two or three times a week. The letters were encouraging. Madame slept well. She had no attacks. Her facial spasms were mild and infrequent.

The journey in mid-February by Dickens and his wife from Rome to Naples caused a hiatus in the reports from Emile de la Rue, but when the letters caught up with Dickens, he knew Augusta was in jeopardy. Emile described sleepless nights and attacks of spasm in his wife. There had been nights when Dickens, himself, sprang awake, filled with the gravest anxiety—anxiety he attributed to Augusta de la Rue. The fears she experienced, she communicated to him through their unique bond. Dickens had done as promised and faithfully stopped his days and nights at the appointed times to concentrate his thoughts on Augusta de la Rue. Emile's earlier letters confirmed his wife's adherence to the same schedule with her either sitting quietly or lying peacefully at those times, often nodding off to sleep afterwards. But of late, de la Rue now wrote, Augusta had ignored her long-range sessions with Dickens, fearful, according to de la Rue, of infecting Dickens with her dread. Her rest, Emile went on, had often been disturbed by a dream of some sort—a dream where she moaned aloud about the presence of a phantom, and her spasms, especially of her left cheek, had returned and frequently left her worn and haggard.

Dickens wrote Emile daily for news and strongly recommended he and his wife meet him in Rome in mid-March. He additionally urged de la Rue to be certain his wife settled down at the times appointed so he could attempt his long-distance treatment of her. De la Rue reported, however, that his wife had taken to leaving the house every morning rather than, according to her, "subject her savior" to the dreadful specter she knew would come to haunt him because of her. De la Rue further reported his wife's pacing the floor until the time for the nightly session passed.

Dickens wrote to Emile of the phantom, "I cannot beat it down, or keep it down, at a distance" and repeated his insistence that the couple travel to meet him. He wrote to Augusta de la Rue promising to shatter the phantom "like glass" if only she would travel to him. De la Rue's first letter of March settled the matter. He promised he and his wife would meet Dickens in Rome at the Hotel Meloni at the beginning of Holy Week.

Catherine Dickens was appalled when she saw her husband lead the de la Rues into the lobby of the Hotel Meloni on March 20th. Dickens, aware of their imminent arrival, had ridden out to usher them into the city. At her first opportunity his wife asked for an explanation.

"What are those people doing here, Charles? You knew they were coming, of course."

"Madame de la Rue has been very ill. Without my

treatments she has regressed. She needs to be treated, Kate. I suggested they join us here in Rome."

"Did it ever cross your mind to consult me about this? Did it ever cross your mind to let me know what you'd done?"

"Kate, the woman needs me to treat her."

"And what is it that you need? Can you tell me that?"

Dickens nearly exploded in anger. Righteously invulnerable in his own mind to the insinuations of his wife and thoroughly aware his relationship with Madame de la Rue was simply one of doctor and patient, he had scant patience for his wife's carryings-on.

"She must be treated and that's an end of it, Kate."

Dickens fixed his wife with a stare so frigid with authority and warning it quieted her. For the time being.

Augusta de la Rue's health soon fell into a pattern. During the day she felt well enough to join Dickens and his wife on their jaunts exploring Rome. Deep into the night, however, her dreams would rise. De la Rue often summoned Dickens from his hotel room, waking Catherine, of course, in the process. Dickens, clad in his nightclothes and robe, would hurry to the de la Rue's rooms and quiet Madame de la Rue so she could sleep through the rest of the night. With de la Rue pacing anxiously outside the door and Catherine waiting back in their bed, Dickens found no opportunity to probe further into the story of the phantom and the ring. He returned to his room drained, yet unable to return to sleep. He paced the bedroom, sometimes until dawn, engendering the profound disapproval of his wife.

Dickens learned in Rome of his wife's pregnancy.

Their sixth child would eventually to be named Alfred D'Orsay Tennyson Dickens. Kate's pregnancies had all been difficult ones—more so psychologically than physically—and Dickens imagined her hysteria over Madame de la Rue sprang from her condition.

The two couples continued to travel the countryside around Rome together daily, finally arriving back in Genoa April 9. Dickens wrote of mesmerizing Madame de la Rue as they traveled "sometimes under olive trees, sometimes in vineyards, sometimes in the traveling carriage, sometimes in wayside inns during the midday halt." He did so hoping to alleviate the need for late night visits to the de la Rue rooms, but when the visits were necessary, he went.

Finally, in mid-April, back at the Peschiere, Catherine Dickens had had enough. Thirty years old and about to bear Dickens his sixth child, she told herself that *she* was his wife; not Madame Augusta de la Rue.

"This must stop," she demanded as she and her husband stood in their bedroom.

Dickens stared at her.

"You must stop seeing this woman." Tears dropped down her cheeks.

"She is a sick..."

"Don't tell me about her sickness. You have a wife. You have me. I am going to have another of your babies. Give me the time that you give to her. I know what is going on between you. I can see it. I can feel it. I can see the signs. I *know* it. Even if her husband is willing to share, your wife is not."

Dickens nostrils flared and his stare grew lethal.

"If you want her, take her. Move in with them. I don't care. Her husband apparently doesn't care what you two do together, but I care and I want it *stopped*." Catherine pounded her thighs with her fists to emphasize her point. Her voice, like her emotions, grew wild and out of control.

"I am merely curing her of a disease."

"Let someone else *merely* do it. You *will* stop going to her. You *will* stop. You will tell them that I *forbid* it."

"Kate," Dickens said in a measured tone," you've already embarrassed me by scarcely speaking to them on the trip here from Rome..."

"Embarrassed? If embarrassment means anything to you—if embarrassment is something that is not to be tolerated, think of *my* embarrassment. My husband—night after night—alone in another woman's bedroom—visiting her at all hours—her husband out of the house. No, no, no." Catherine fell on the bed and beat at the counterpane with her fists. "You will tell them," she mumbled into the mix of bedding she had disarranged, "or I will leave. I will take the children and leave right now. I will. I will."

Dickens turned and left the room.

The next day, seeing no way out of his dilemma with his wife, he visited Emile de la Rue in his office and explained about his wife's pregnancy and her feelings. Dickens told him it would be necessary to slacken his attentions to Madame de la Rue's disease. He hoped Emile would explain all of this to his wife. Dickens vowed he would visit when he could, but they could no longer expect his appearance according to any set schedule, and there could be no more distress calls after dark.

De la Rue, of course, had noted Catherine's behavior as they traveled and so this visit from Dickens did not come as too great a surprise. He told Dickens he understood, and it would have no effect on their friendship or the regard both he and his wife felt for both him and his wife.

Dickens left the meeting as angry as he could ever remember being.

Dickens described his next six weeks as "lying back on sofas and leaning out of windows and over balconies, in a sort of mild intoxication." He would visit the Brignole Rosso on occasion to treat Augusta de la Rue, but all in all, he had nothing to do and nothing to write other than letters, and he longed for home.

Dickens made plans to leave Genoa on June 9 and travel back home via Zurich, Frankfurt, Cologne and Brussels. As the departure date neared, the Peschiere became a madhouse of boxes, organizing, packing, with a swirl of workmen and children underfoot.

When Dickens mentioned the situation to Emile de la Rue, Emile offered him the hospitality of his home. Dickens accepted his offer with two things on his mind he wished to accomplish. First, he did not want to leave Catherine with the impression she could control his behavior. The visit to Emile de la Rue, which she had forced upon him, had humiliated him. Secondly, he wanted a final opportunity to probe into Augusta's story of the phantom and ring. If only he could be clear about what plagued her, it was still not too late, he believed, to eradicate her debilitating dreams forever. He told Catherine of his decision, honestly admitting he wanted both to avoid the chaos of the Peschiere and make one last attempt at curing Madame de la Rue. Catherine, unable to match wills with her husband a second time, simply turned away and went back about her business.

Before Dickens left for two nights at the Brignole Rosso, he wrote a letter to his wife and left it on her pillow. He explained the embarrassment she had put him through and vowed an oath to the Almighty that his relationship with Augusta de la Rue was innocent. He went on, "...the intense pursuit of any idea that takes complete possession of me, is one of the qualities that makes me different—sometimes for good; sometimes I dare say for evil—from other men.

"Whatever (is making you) unhappy...(has) no other root, beginning, middle, or end, than whatever has made you proud and honored in your married life and gives you station better than rank, surrounded you with many enviable things. This is the plain truth, and here I leave it.

"You have it in your power to set it right at once by writing a note to say...you couldn't receive her remembrance (Madame de la Rue had sent Catherine a floral arrangement a few days earlier 'to make your final days in Genoa as pleasant as possible') without a desire to respond—and that if you should ever meet again you hope it will be for a friendly association without any sort of shadow upon it. I shall never ask whether you have done this or not and shall never approach the subject from this hour."

With this attempt to provide closure to his wife's jealousy, Dickens left the Peschiere for the de la Rues.

Chapter Eleven

Dickens lunched with the de la Rues on Saturday, June 7 and then, as Dickens had privately suggested, de la Rue left the house to go to his office so Dickens could administer a treatment to his wife. Dickens remained intent on bringing a resolution to Madame de la Rue's malady as well as satisfaction to his own curiosity.

"Now that we're alone, Augusta—you're aware Emile knows of your phantom and of your dreams?"

Augusta looked down and then back at Dickens and nodded. "Yes. He's told me what I mumble in the midst of my seizures."

"I believe we were...are very close to dispelling the phantom and those dreams, and I would like to use these two days to try."

Augusta breathed a deep, uncertain sigh. "I am so afraid for you, Charles. I sense harm coming to you from this." She looked away, ashamed. "That is why I avoided our sessions when you traveled. I know you're in danger."

Dickens waved her fears away. "I fear nothing of the sort. My only desire is to affect a cure for you. I know I can and with your help, I will. There is so little time left. No harm can come to me in so short a time."

She could no more stand up to Dickens' will, face-to-face with him, than Catherine or anyone else could. She consented saying, "The house is quiet and empty." The servants, unless kept on for a party of some sort, were free after lunch on Saturday. "We can begin here and now." They sat together on a sofa in the sitting room. Dickens rose and pulled over a chair so he could face her.

"Your phantom springs from your time in Rome when...the accident occurred."

Augusta lifted her head higher, no longer casually agreeable to Dickens' desires.

Dickens saw and lifted a calm hand to her. "It is true. I know it to be so."

Augusta looked at him, waiting.

"I hope to relieve you of the fears springing from that time."

Dickens began to make passes with his hands and to invite the woman to the safe place where they could speak honestly. In less than four minutes Augusta de la Rue had reached trance.

Dickens asked many of the same questions he had asked before. Augusta's answers remained constant. Most importantly, she insisted she had seen the ring in the phantom's room.

"Was it your brother's room where you saw the ring?"

Augusta refused to answer.

"Where are you now?" Dickens asked.

"With you. In the safe place."

"What do you see?"

She paused. "We are on a hill. There are people in the distance."

"How many people?"

"I see three people." Augusta's eyelids fluttered open briefly and dropped shut.

"Do you recognize those people?"

"Yes."

"Who are they?'

"My brother Charles. Rodney." She stopped.

"Who is the third?"

She would not answer.

"What are the people doing?"

"One is leading Rodney away."

"Is it your brother who is leading Rodney away?"

Dickens thought he saw the woman move her head to indicate "no," but the movement was so slight he could not be certain.

"Who is left standing on the hill?"

"You and I are there."

"Where is the third figure left behind when the other two left?"

"Gone. Where is my brother?" Augusta spoke in a painful voice and Dickens took a few moments to quiet her.

"You've told me of Emile's kindness to you at this time."

"Yes, he was very kind."

"How often did you see him?"

"Every day."

"You saw Emile every day?"

"Yes."

"What happened when your brother came back from the hike and reported Rodney missing?"

It took three repetitions of the question to elicit a fearful, agitated response. Dickens, as usual, held the woman's hand and felt her squeeze tightly upon his own.

108

"I went to find Emile."

"And what did he say?"

"He was not in his room."

"When did you finally speak to him?"

"When he returned a short time later."

"What did he do?"

"He waited with us for Rodney to return."

"And when Rodney did not return, what did he do?"

"He summoned the authorities. My father was too upset. They searched. They searched. My brother couldn't explain...oh, where is my brother?"

Augusta dropped Dickens' hand and stood up. He took her by the shoulders, fearful he had ignited something within her he would be unable to extinguish. Gradually he relaxed her, sat her down, and awakened her.

"You've made me tired, Charles," she said, putting her hand to her right temple.

"We are so close, Augusta. Let me help you rest. Come." Dickens led her into the bedroom. Augusta lay down and in a few minutes, he had her sleeping peacefully. He watched over her for a while, then left.

Dickens, confident the woman would be safe, went to de la Rue's office. Emile was there alone and greeted him with alarm.

"Augusta, is she...?"

Dickens smiled with a calmness he did not feel. "She is well. I'd like to speak with you."

"Certainly."

Emile walked to a cabinet and took out a bottle of red wine along with two wineglasses. He opened the bottle and poured.

Dickens took a glass and said, "Emile, your wife is haunted—there is no better word—by a phantom who violates her dreams. What happens to her physically is simply a manifestation of the torment she feels mentally. I believe the source of this phantom, which you've heard her mention, can be found in the occurrences of ten years ago when the accident happened to the young man named Rodney Dowd."

De la Rue's glass stopped on its way to his mouth. He wet his lips with his tongue before sipping some of his wine.

Dickens studied the man as he continued. "She doesn't consciously acknowledge this, understand it, or think about it, but I'm certain deep within her it is the source of her misery. I have a theory and I am hoping you will tell me what you remember about that time. Perhaps you can provide me with the information I need to relieve her of this torment."

De la Rue sipped some more wine and set his glass down on his desk. "Of course."

Dickens noted that for an instant de la Rue could not bring himself to meet his eyes.

"Where should I begin?"

"Begin with meeting your future wife."

"Well, we were in Turin. I was on my way to Egypt where I stayed for a month or so on bank business. I met the family again in Rome, where they had traveled as soon as I departed. I remember delaying my departure for Egypt to coincide with their departure for Rome."

"Had you fallen in love with your wife by then?"

Dickens saw a small vertical line form above the bridge of de la Rue's nose.

"I had. Yes."

"And she?"

"She? Perhaps not."

"Go on, if you will. When did you meet this Rodney Dowd?"

"In Rome. Augusta had known him briefly before, and he was a suitor of hers. Gave her gifts. Gloves, I remember." De la Rue smiled. "Endless pairs of gloves. He was having a portrait of her painted, but it was never completed. Augusta could not bring herself to sit for it after the accident."

"Will you tell me about the argument you heard before the accident?"

De la Rue smiled again. "Charles, you astonish me."

Dickens could see the banker had relaxed and settled into his tale with an assurance absent at its start.

Dickens, not to be outdone, assumed a nonchalance. "Angus mentioned it."

"To be sure. I heard a disagreement. Augusta's brother told the Dowd boy why he opposed his marrying his sister. They had quite an animated discussion."

"Had there been such arguments before?"

"From what I heard, it was not the first time the topic had come up between them."

"And so the two young men went walking next day and only one returned?"

"Yes."

"And Augusta turned to you for support?"

"I was...nearby. Her father was frantic. Someone had to take charge of the situation."

"Her father was worried about his son, no doubt."

"No doubt."

"And Augusta turned to you?" Dickens repeated.

"We grew quite close. As you can see."

"It is your wife's concern—perhaps belief—that her brother caused the other young man's disappearance and this is, I believe, the source of her sufferings."

"Circumstances were black against him. But can you not remove this thorn from her mind?"

"I will try again. Tomorrow. I know I will succeed, Emile."

Emile refilled the two glasses and lifted his toward Dickens. "To your success."

Dickens lifted his glass in return, and the conversation moved elsewhere.

As they subsequently decided, Emile de la Rue left the Brignole Rosso the next morning so Dickens could be alone with his wife. The cook was due back to prepare lunch, but she would be a floor below the sitting room where Dickens and Augusta de la Rue worked.

Augusta smiled as Dickens pulled up a chair. "Is it now or never, Charles?"

"Unfortunately, it is," Dickens said, painting a smile on his face.

"You have helped me so much already."

"After today you will be cured."

The woman grimaced, indicating she thought this a dubious assurance.

Dickens began and soon the woman reached trance. His only goal was to remove or at least alleviate the guilt Augusta felt over her brother's exile.

"Your brother did not want you to marry Rodney. Why?"

"But he did."

"I'm sorry. Who did?"

"My brother did. He did want me to marry Rodney."

Dickens was confused.

"The night before the accident your brother had an argument with Rodney and told him he did not want you to marry him."

Augusta sat stock still for a moment. Then her head went side to side twice.

"Was there no argument?"

"The night before the accident my brother took me to task for the attentions I paid to Emile."

"Emile!"

"Yes." The woman's respiration quickened.

Dickens reminded the woman they were in the safe place where she could tell him anything, and gradually her breathing settled back into a regular rhythm.

"What did your brother tell you?"

"He told me Emile had had many other women. And opium. He knew Emile used opium."

"Emile smoked opium?"

"Yes. My brother knew. After we married, Emile admitted it to me and he stopped."

"Go on."

"My brother told me Emile was insincere and too old

for me. He said Rodney loved me truly and planned to ask me to marry him the next day after he and my brother had spent the morning hiking together. Then my brother described the ring to me. But Emile loves me truly. He does. He does."

Dickens calmed her. "Of course he does, Augusta. He helped you get through that difficult period."

"Yes, he was there all the time."

"He visited you every day, did he?"

"No."

"No?"

"He stayed with us. In my brother's room. My brother moved to a smaller room in the house."

Dickens felt a black chill creep over him.

"Emile lived in the house all of this time?" Dickens searched his memory.

"Yes. He stayed with us in Rome."

"Where was he the day of the accident?"

"I looked for him but he did not return until after Charles."

"Tell me again about the ring you saw."

The woman clamped her fingers tightly around Dickens' hand.

"I saw the ring. In his room."

"In whose room did you see the ring?"

"The phantom's. The phantom who has been frightening me." The woman's voice rose and her eyes opened. "The phantom had the ring."

Dickens patiently calmed Augusta. He would not stop until he knew. He tried the question another way.

"Tell me about how you saw the ring."

Augusta began to breathe rapidly.

"We are in the safe place. You can tell me, Augusta."

"Emile came home in the afternoon and learned Rodney was missing. He did not leave my side until evening when we knew something had gone terribly wrong. The authorities came to the house. Emile went into his room. I spoke to my father for a moment. Then I went into my brother's room to look for Emile. His room. He was not there. On the floor under his dresser I saw the ring. The ring! How it shone. Rubies and diamonds. It lay on the floor. The ring my brother had described. I ran from the room. I was frightened. I went back to my father. A moment later Emile joined us. I left and returned to Emile's room, but the ring was no longer there. Emile. Emile had the ring. He took it from Rodney when he...when he..." Augusta shot to her feet and screamed, then slumped back onto the sofa.

Dickens' heart beat a fearful staccato as he tried to compose both the woman and himself. Into his memory flashed the image of the wineglass pausing on its way to Emile's mouth that afternoon and the tiny furrow forming between his eyes. He recalled Emile wetting his lips with his tongue and averting his eyes for a moment. And what had he said? "I was nearby." He had said it hesitantly, hiding the fact he was *living* in the house. In the brother's room. Where Augusta saw the ring. Dickens recalled the growing assurance Emile displayed in telling his story when he realized Dickens was on a wrong track. Emile had done it. Emile had murdered young Rodney Dowd. Dickens was certain of it.

It took fifteen minutes to return Augusta to quiet trance. It took another fifteen for him to formulate what would have to pass for a solution.

"Augusta, you did not see the ring the night of the accident. You saw the ring the day before the accident. Rodney gave the ring to Charles for him to admire. Charles left it on his dresser for a moment. It fell on the floor, and you saw it roll under the dresser. Charles had the ring. It was the day before the accident when you saw the ring under the dresser." On and on Dickens went. He made the woman repeat the mantra after him. The day before—Charles had the ring.

Finally, he let her sleep.

Dickens mind whirled. He realized Augusta knew deep within that, because he had the ring, Emile had been involved in the disappearance of Rodney Dowd. She did not tell the authorities he had the ring. She protected him. She did not contradict Emile's story to the authorities about the argument the night before. Emile *had* overheard a conversation, a conversation between Charles and his sister in which Charles defamed Emile's character and revealed Rodney's intent to propose marriage the next day. Emile then took steps to prevent Rodney from testing Augusta's affection for him. Emile had also learned of the ring in this conversation.

Emile de la Rue was the phantom who haunted Augusta's dreams. In an intimate, hidden place where she never ventured with her conscious mind, she stored the knowledge that her husband gained her hand through murder.

116

She had protected the man at the expense of her brother's reputation and exile. She had protected him so she could have him for a husband. Emile de la Rue's despicable behavior had caused the terrible pain and guilt inside his wife.

De la Rue's behavior lit a vengeful fire inside Dickens. He immediately decided he would not spend another night under this accursed roof, but before he left he would confront Emile de la Rue.

Chapter Twelve

After Dickens sufficiently digested what he had heard and plotted his coming behavior, he awoke Augusta de la Rue.

Her eyes fluttered open, clear, blue, and lovely as always.

"How do you feel?" Dickens asked, his voice calm, his emotions now under control.

She smiled. "I feel fine, Charles. Fine."

"We've made wonderful progress since Christmas."

"All because of you." She moved her hand to Dickens' arm. "Thank you."

Dickens averted his eyes and stood. "I'll be going back to the Peschiere shortly."

"You're not staying with us tonight?"

Dickens shook his head. "I'd planned to but I have things I must do before we leave tomorrow. And Kate would like me home."

"Ah." Augusta looked away momentarily.

"I'll gather my things, but I do want to speak with Emile before I leave. I want him to know I appreciate what he's done."

"Of course."

Dickens went to his bedroom and packed the few things he had brought with him from the Peschiere.

Emile de la Rue returned home moments before the call to lunch, forcing Dickens to dine with Monsieur and

Madame de la Rue. The conversation revolved around Dickens' imminent departure and common memories the three had established over the past year. The nearer lunch came to an end—the nearer the time for him to confront de la Rue—the greater rose Dickens' righteous anger within him. Finally, the servant cleared the dishes.

Emile complimented his wife. "You look wonderful, darling. The day is beautiful. Why don't we walk down to the water after seeing Charles home?"

"I'd like to speak with you, Emile. Alone," Dickens interrupted.

"I'll walk by myself a while." Augusta rose and touched her husband's shoulder. "Meet me outside the church when you finish. Half-an-hour?"

De la Rue walked his wife to the apartment door and saw her out.

"Now, what is it Charles?"

Dickens remained standing and fixed his eyes on de la Rue, who settled comfortably in a chair. He crossed his legs and threw an arm leisurely across the back of the chair.

"I told you—and you know from your wife herself—that a phantom haunts her dreams. This phantom is the cause of all her ill health."

De la Rue listened attentively.

"I've discovered the source of those dreams and the identity of this phantom."

"Go on." De la Rue uncrossed his legs, resettled himself in the chair, and crossed his legs again.

Dickens' eyes bored fearlessly into Emile's. "The disappearance of this young man, Rodney Dowd, was no accident."

"What do you mean?" Except for his eyes narrowing, Emile did not move.

"Augusta saw the ruby and diamond ring in your possession, Emile. You dropped it momentarily on the floor beneath the dresser in her brother's room, where you stayed. Surely you recall. It isn't likely you'd forget such a thing. Your wife saw it lying there on the evening of the...murder."

De la Rue's lips tightened and he crossed his arms over his chest.

"She saw the ring in your room and deep within her she knows the only way the ring could have come into your possession was if you'd taken it from the young man himself, which you did when, in some manner known only to you, you made away with him."

"Why would I want...?"

"Emile! Don't insult me and degrade yourself even more in my eyes than you have already. You knew the young man planned to propose to Augusta. You overheard the conversation the night before between Augusta and her brother. The two young men never argued. You were afraid she would accept the young man. Because of your *love* for her..." Dickens voice dripped sarcasm. "...because of your love for her, I say, you wanted to be certain he never had that chance. You wanted to be certain you were her only suitor."

De la Rue rose from his chair and walked toward a table against the wall. He opened a drawer.

Dickens tensed.

De la Rue extracted a cigar. He walked calmly back to his chair and fussed with his cigar before lighting it.

Dickens' detestation of the man bubbled over.

"Having seen the ring, Augusta knew what you had done but did nothing about it, and because she did nothing you went unpunished. The punishment for your act, Emile, has fallen on *her*. Her brother has been lost to her, and she is now burdened with this terrible affliction, which I hope to God I have been able to cure. She protected you—heaven knows why—and she has been suffering the consequences of her decision for all of these long years."

De la Rue blew a mouthful of smoke in Dickens' direction.

"I don't believe you," he said, looking straight at Dickens. "My wife has never intimated any knowledge remotely like what you have described."

"Your wife *cannot* allow herself to acknowledge such an act on your part. She *cannot* have such an understanding be a part of her daily consciousness. I fear it would kill her if she were forced to acknowledge it. If I were to tell her now what I know to be true, she would deny it out of sheer necessity—her necessity to survive, but the understanding is within her. It causes her dreams. It is embodied in this phantom. The phantom is you, Emile. You." Dickens' voice rose. "You haunt your wife's dreams, terrorizing her, ravaging her mind and her health. You. You." Dickens pointed at de la Rue, his right hand shaking with fury, his righteous and unshakable moral certainty meeting head-on with De la Rue's arrogant and unshakable certainty that nothing could weaken his wife's attachment to him.

De la Rue drew in another mouthful of smoke and held it, gazing scornfully at Dickens the while. He exhaled and said, "Your possessing such knowledge leaves you where, Charles? Augusta has been a true and faithful wife all these years. We love each other. We enjoy each other. And she is—except for her occasional attacks—a happy woman. We do not have a marriage like some—full of suspicion...and boredom."

Dickens knew Emile referred to him and Kate and restrained himself from leaping on the man.

"Except for her occasional attacks?" Dickens shot back angrily. "You have caused these attacks. You are the source of these attacks. Do not sit there and act as if your wife's attacks are but a small price to pay to possess the likes of you! You talk as if you were some rare and precious prize. What you have done is to destroy the woman's peace of mind, her health, and her stability."

"I have gained a beautiful, charming, loyal woman. How many of us can say the same?"

Dickens took a step forward but de la Rue merely smiled.

"Charles, Augusta is waiting. Let's meet her. We will walk you home, and then you and I will never have to see one another again."

Dickens started for the door, his mind full of curses aching to explode into de la Rue's ears. He spun about. "You, sir, are a despicable, degraded monster. A murderer without the morality of a common dog. No animal in its most predatory moment would behave in a like manner to you. I want you to live the rest of your life with my opinion of you ringing in your ears. You are filth, Emile. Filth. Something any respectable man would wipe from his boots. Stay here. I will go and say good-bye to your wife and tell her you will be along directly. We *will* never see one another again because I refuse to let my eyes rest upon the sight of you." Dickens spun back toward the door. He took a few steps, paused, and slowly turned back to de la Rue.

"Someday, somehow, Emile, I will find a way to reveal your crime to the world. I promise you this. One day the world will know you for the despicable murderer you are. As the Almighty is my witness, I promise you this." He turned away and left the room.

He bolted down the stairs to the street and strode off in the direction of the church. Augusta de la Rue paced patiently in the bright sunshine before the church when Dickens arrived. She smiled a greeting. "Where is Emile?"

Dickens responded with as cheery a greeting as he could muster. "He will be along directly. I didn't want to wait. I must be getting back home. But, Augusta, I want to wish you well and farewell. If ever you need a friend, a councilor, you may depend on me. Write. Let me know how you are. I hope and pray you will be well."

"I know I will be, Charles. And, again, all thanks to you."

They clasped hands a moment, and Dickens walked off toward the Peschiere.

Dickens and his family were back in London in his Devonshire Terrace home in early July 1845. Over the next few years Dickens received occasional letters, penned by Emile de la Rue but written clearly at his wife's urging. She was well; her attacks infrequent; her gratitude eternal. Gradually, though, the letters dropped off and finally ceased altogether, and Dickens had no further contact with the de la Rues until the evening in the Athenaeum Club when Emile de la Rue had boldly approached Dickens' table.

Dickens rose and stared from a window for a brief spell. He turned to Forster and said, "And so what do you think, John? Madame de la Rue showed dreadful judgment in that one moment, but she was a girl then of barely eighteen. What a shock it must have been. How confusing and overwhelming for her. The time for action, for her speaking out, passed quickly, and soon it was too late. She was engaged to the man.

"But it is he, John, he who is the villain in all of this. A murderer. The cause of his wife's every distress." Dickens threw himself back into his chair and vaulted onward not giving Forster time to respond.

"I will have him now, John. I had no way to touch him back in Genoa out of consideration for his wife; the truth, I know, would have killed her. And what proof could I offer? No legal authority anywhere would have accepted the seemingly mad dreams of a woman as evidence of a murder ten years in the past, but what she dreamed *was* the truth, John; truth she buried as deep as human heart can bury anything. But Augusta is gone. She can be hurt no longer, so there is nothing to stop me any longer from unmasking the man she married. I have an obligation to do so."

"What are you planning?" Forster said, knowing it

had something to do with the story Dickens had proposed.

"I will exact vengeance through my story. I will put his crime into my story. I will taunt him with details only he will recognize. He will know the end of his great game is coming and will be unable to stop it. I will make him suffer as he made her suffer."

"Charles, it is hardly good for your health to get so worked up."

"My health be damned," Dickens growled. "I will taunt him in my story and in the final episode I will state it right out—just as Hamlet does before Claudius."

The smile on Dickens' face—a smile that burned rather than beamed—chilled Forster.

"This murder was done in the fashion of a murder committed in Rome in 1834, and the name of the murderer is Emile de la Rue!"

The two men sat in silence for a moment.

"Let's return to the house, John. There is plenty of time before dinner for a drink, and I think I would like one."

Forster, unable to form a suitable response and knowing any response other than total agreement with Dickens would be ignored anyway, agreed. It was long past time for a drink.

Chapter Thirteen

March 3, 1870. Despite his failing health Charles Dickens remained as busy as ever. He submitted himself to the weekly grind of editing *All The Year Round* even as he composed the fourth number of *The Mystery of Edwin Drood*, whose first number would not be published until March 31, as well as undertaking a series of twelve public readings from his works. A year earlier Dickens' doctors, Frank Beard and Thomas Watson, had forbidden the continuation of a tour of readings, convinced the struggle to summon the energy he expended during these readings was literally killing him. Dickens had no choice but to comply with their demand, but a few months later, much improved and feeling guilty for Chappell and Company's—the tour sponsor—financial loss when the readings were canceled, he petitioned his doctors to allow him a final series of farewell readings. They agreed, albeit with a number of demands: he must wait until the new year began and read no more than a dozen times, and all the readings must take place in London at Saint James Hall with Dr. Beard in attendance. Dickens did not mind the prescription against railway travel, which had become a terror and torment to him since nearly losing his life in the horrific Staplehurst train derailment in 1865. The car he rode in was the first car not to go plunging down a deadly embankment. They finally settled on two readings per week in the second half of January and one per week on Tuesdays in February and March.

Dickens had closed Gad's Hill in early 1870 and, along with daughter Mamie and sister-in-law Georgina, taken lodgings in London at 5 Hyde Park Place through May to eliminate the need for any travel whatsoever. Now only two readings remained, March 8 and March 15, and he discussed these final appearances with John Forster as the two men walked down Oxford Street.

"You should give up that one selection, Charles," Forster advised. "You know you must."

"It's my best piece of material. You know it is," Dickens mimicked with a smile.

"Best piece or not, Sikes killing Nancy on stage... you know what you're like after that reading."

The two men were silent. They both knew what Dickens was like after any of his readings, *especially* the one he had drawn from *The Adventures of Oliver Twist.* He would lie prostrate on his dressing room sofa, his pulse racing as high as 125, Dr. Beard at his side ministering to him, Charley his son, Ellen his mistress, his daughters Mamie and Kate hovering near, full of concern.

"There are only two left before I disappear from the stage forever. But, John, there's nothing in the world equal to seeing the house rise at you, one sea of delighted faces, one hurrah of applause! I will miss my creations. I will miss it all," he said softly.

"Beard has told Charley he won't be responsible if you simply drop down dead during a performance."

Dickens chuckled. "I don't think it likely, John. Next Tuesday I will read from *Twist* one last time. My final readings will be the *Carol* and the trial from *Pickwick.*"

Although Forster counted arguing as one of his greatest talents, he knew better than to argue with Dickens.

Dickens pointed. "Look. There's Iron-headed Polly." Iron-headed Polly was one of London's ubiquitous costermongers. Penny pork pies were Polly's specialty. Polly had come by her name when another costermonger tried to commandeer her corner at Oxford and Baker Streets and a battle ensued. The enemy had whacked Polly across the head with an iron pot to little effect. Polly then snatched the pot from the man's hand and delivered him a sound thrashing with it. Disputes over the proprietorship of the corner ceased forevermore.

"Two today, Polly," said Dickens. "Business is going well for you, I hope."

"Very 'ard livin' on what I has live on, Mr. D." She wrapped two pies and handed them to Dickens, who would take them to his office. She grinned. "But's allus good to sells to you, Mr. D." She knew Dickens would no more leave her with a mere two pence than he would steal the pies from her.

Dickens took a shilling from his pocket and handed it to the ragged woman.

"You make the best pies in London, Polly."

The woman cackled and stuffed the shilling deep down somewhere in her clothing.

"Where's your little Joey?" Dickens asked.

"Tobaccy hunt." Polly's young son, Joey—some eight years old—searched the streets of London for discarded cigar butts. He collected them, salvaged as much usable tobacco as he could, and sold the tobacco to the poor.

"For Joey." Dickens handed the woman a wad of newspaper which contained a week's collection of cigar butts Dickens had saved along with another shilling.

Iron-headed Polly cackled again and nodded vigorously.

"Allus good to sells to you, Mr. D."

Dickens and Forster crossed Baker Street.

Dickens turned to Forster. "We part here. I'll see you at Blanchard's tonight, of course, for Ellen's birthday dinner."

"I'll be there," Forster promised. He watched Dickens settle the collar of his great coat about his neck and turn down Baker Street toward the *All The Year Round* offices.

Forster walked on to Bond Street and turned right toward Pall Mall and the Athenaeum to lunch with Mark Lemon, the editor of *Punch,* but Dickens preyed on his mind. Four weeks from this very day the first number of *Drood* would be in the bookstores. Dickens had read the first three numbers to him and a few select others, in Forster's home. No one but he, of course, understood the references to Dickens' time in Genoa and his tremendous and awful discovery there, but stroke by stroke Dickens filled his book's canvas with images of that time. Forster recognized many of them but doubtless there were others to be understood by de la Rue only.

Forster had tried to talk Dickens out of his mad scheme, but Dickens had rarely been talked out of anything he had set his mind to, and he had set his mind irreversibly on exposing Emile de la Rue.

A good crowd filled the coffee room at the Athenaeum. Mark Lemon, a rotund and bearded image of Sir

John Falstaff, whom in fact he had played in one of Dickens' numerous theatrical endeavors, waited for Forster at a table. Also seated at the table were Lord Allsgood and Emile de la Rue.

The eyes of Forster and de la Rue found each other immediately, and immediately the loathing Dickens felt for de la Rue filled Forster. Smugness and arrogance exuded from the impeccably dressed man. In his mind Forster could again hear Dickens' voice rise in anger when he repeated what he had said to de la Rue at their last encounter in Italy those twenty-five years earlier. "Do not sit there and act as if your wife's attacks are but a small price to pay to possess the likes of you! You talk as if you were some rare and precious prize." Rare and precious prize, indeed, Forster thought. The eyes of the two men refused to disengage. Forster, his pugnacious jaw jutting out as the memory of Dickens' anger swelled his own, approached the table as the other three men rose.

"John," said Mark Lemon, "you know Lord Allsgood, of course. Have you met Emile de la Rue? He's taken one of Lord Allsgood's properties, The Kensington."

Forster moved toward the empty chair opposite de la Rue. He would not shake the man's hand if he could avoid it.

"Yes, we've met." De la Rue smiled and offered his hand. "We have a friend in common. Mr. Dickens."

"Of course," said Lemon.

Forster stiffly grasped de la Rue's hand, pumped it once, and let it go. De la Rue's eyes wandered as Forster's bore into him.

Lemon spoke. "I was just telling them of the party

Charles is giving tonight. Charles, I know, would be pleased if Lord Allsgood would stop by at least for a drink. With Mr. de la Rue, of course."

Forster steeled himself, wondering whether Lemon could have possibly have suggested anything Dickens would have wanted less.

"To be sure," Forster responded gruffly. "I think though, Mark, it's best to keep this dinner a private affair. The circumstances and all."

"Ah." De la Rue tilted his head back momentarily. "The young actress, yes. I understand."

The "young actress" was Ellen Ternan, whom Dickens had met nearly thirteen years earlier in August of 1857 when he needed three professional actresses to replace family members and friends when one of his theatrical endeavors, *The Frozen Deep,* moved on to play a large theatre in Manchester. Ellen, her sister Maria, and her mother Frances were the chosen actresses. Ellen was 18 at the time, Dickens 45. This meeting with Ellen brought about a crisis in his increasingly tense marriage. Shortly after meeting Ellen, Dickens had workmen build a wall across his bedroom, adding a physical separation to the psychological and emotional barrier between him and his wife. Nine months later Dickens separated from Catherine and in an acrimonious proceeding fueled by rumors of philandering with Ellen and incest with his sister-in-law, who stayed behind to tend his house and care for the children, Dickens gave Catherine a 600-pound yearly income and never set eyes on her again. Ten months after this permanent separation he bought a home for the Ternan family at 2 Houghton Place,

Ampthill Square in London. When Ellen reached twenty-one, Dickens signed the house over to her as agreed, and Ellen lived there for much the rest of her life. By the 1860's Dickens and she were an open secret.

Forster glared at de la Rue. "She was an actress at one time," he said stiffly.

De la Rue smirked and made a small nod of the head.

An uneasy quiet settled on the table until Lord Allsgood cleared his throat and said, "Well, Emile, I believe we should let our friends enjoy their lunch."

Everyone rose.

"You will give Mr. Dickens my best," said de la Rue.

De la Rue's tone—mocking or simply his perpetual arrogance Forster could not determine—brought Forster's eyes to bear again. He responded with only a curt nod, and de la Rue and Lord Allsgood left the table.

Though he did not show it, this chance meeting with Forster unsettled Emile de la Rue. He had detected an unfounded belligerence in Forster's manner. As de la Rue dined and chatted with Lord Allsgood, the table where Forster and Lemon sat repeatedly drew his eye. Three of those times he noticed Forster staring his way, his bulldog face intent and, to de la Rue's mind, hostile. Why?

De la Rue finished his lunch and left the club. As he paced along Pall Mall, the image of Forster's glaring eyes stayed with him. What reason could Forster have for treating him so? Had he taken his remark about "the young actress" as an affront to Dickens? But, no, Forster had been cool to him from the moment their eyes met. He knew how close Forster and Dickens were. It was common knowledge.

Had Dickens revealed to Forster what occurred in Genoa? If so, had he told all of his acquaintances or only Forster? De la Rue had noticed no alteration in how he had been treated by anyone other than Forster, though.

De la Rue tightened his scarf about his neck and went home, unable to shake the feeling that Dickens might possibly bring him great trouble.

Shortly after midnight, a ragged figure skulked along Upper Swandam Lane, north of the Thames on the east side of London Bridge. The figure, a man, passed close to the buildings, trying to blend into the darkest part of the vile and filthy neighborhood. The man heard a scream and paused to watch a man with a grizzled beard in a dark cap pull roughly at a woman he had sent sprawling to the ground. The skulking figure turned into a quiet alley and walked to its end. He came to a solid wooden door, lifted a knocker shaped like a maniacal looking imp, and banged it twice, hard.

The door opened slightly and an old woman peered out.

"I want pipes," came the voice of Emile de la Rue.

The old woman opened the door wider and de la Rue smelled the aroma of opium. He inhaled and moved forward.

From behind the woman a tall, well-muscled Lascar wearing a patch over his left eye appeared. He put his hand against de la Rue's chest.

The old woman creaked, "Got money, luv? Ya needs money, shillin's and pounds, to come in here, dearie."

"Yes, yes." De la Rue drew a pound note from his pocket.

The Lascar lowered his hand and the old woman opened the door wider.

De la Rue entered and saw four or five rooms through the smoke. In each room opium smokers reclined in all manner of positions on filthy cots.

The old woman pointed to an empty cot in one of the rooms.

"Ya gets more 'n one pipe for a pound, dearie. More 'n two even. Lie down'n I'll get chur first."

De la Rue threw his coat toward the head of the cot and lay down. The old woman returned quickly with a pipe. De la Rue took it, savored its appearance for a moment, and began to smoke.

He closed his eyes and before long he had left London behind in a cloud of opium smoke. He was back in Genoa with Augusta. They were young and so deeply in love he knew for a certainty their love would stretch into eternity. He and Augusta together forever. A strange face floated before him. The face of a young man. He concentrated until the face disappeared. Accompanied by a fearful scream, the face had disappeared once before. When it did, Augusta was his.

His second pipe took him deeper and deeper into the past. Augusta had seen the ring. He had not known that fact for all the years of their marriage until Dickens had told him so. Augusta had never mentioned it. Ever. Not at the moment or any time afterward. Had she really seen it? How could she have? But he *had* dropped the ring and exactly where Dickens reported it. Yet, Augusta never gave the slightest indication she had seen the ring—unless, as Dickens claimed, her illness...damn the ring. Damn that man.

Like a resplendent flower bursting open in glorious sunshine, Augusta's face appeared before him as elegant as when they had met. So beautiful. The face of a woman he had to possess. He would have done anything. Anything. The face of a young man floated before his eyes again. He concentrated on Augusta.

His third pipe took him to a place of swirling images. The narrative of his dreams faded into chaos. Rome. Genoa. Augusta. His and Dickens' last meeting in Genoa, an image he pushed aside. Rome. Genoa. Augusta. In love. In love. Augusta. In love.

The pipe dropped from De la Rue's hand as he fell unconscious.

Chapter Fourteen

When Emile de la Rue first saw Augusta, it seemed as if the rest of life stepped aside to make room for the great love he felt for her. She became his first thought upon awakening and a constant dreamy presence throughout the day. His last thoughts before sleep were of her and in sleep she filled his dreams. He had to have her. A necessary trip to Egypt—a tortured month away from her—merely honed his desire and determination to possess her. He vowed to go to any length to accomplish his goal. And he had.

Fear of Charles Dickens began to spread through de la Rue's conscious hours seeming, ironically, to force the rest of his life to step aside as his fear needed room to expand. He could think of little else. The brief but foreboding confrontation with John Forster daunted him. He relived it repeatedly. Forster's eyes; his reluctant handshake; his sharp defense of Dickens' mistress; his belligerent glares while dining. What could it mean? Possibly nothing if Dickens had kept his secret, but possibly everything if Forster knew the secret. And if Forster knew, others might know. Soon, perhaps, everyone would know.

His wife gone, his wealth assured, de la Rue wanted nothing more than to settle in England and live in society. Genoa had been so long ago that he gave no thought to Dickens when he accepted Lord Allsgood's invitation to lease The Kensington. He knew Allsgood needed the income and charged him an excessive rent, but he could depend on the

Lord to be his entrée into the clubs and gatherings of the finest people. This had been his only consideration. The money was irrelevant.

Now, everywhere he went he saw Dickens' face staring out at him from bookstore windows on placards announcing his readings. Daily, de la Rue made the journey back and forth between the offices of *All The Year Round* and 5 Hyde Park Place, trying to get a glimpse of the man. He had half a mind to confront Dickens. Dickens, though, did not seem the type to take kindly to a threat. De la Rue did not want to force Dickens into committing the very act he hoped to prevent.

Dickens, however, could not be found. Unknown to de la Rue, Dickens had gone with Ellen Ternan to Peckham, a town not far from London, where he had rented her a house the day after her birthday dinner. He would not return until Monday, March 7, to prepare for the next night's reading.

Finally, de la Rue decided to purchase one of the few tickets available for Dickens' penultimate reading. He had to get a look at the man. He had to decide whether Dickens loomed as a threat or not.

Tuesday, March 8. Emile de la Rue settled into the next to last row in St. James Hall. He did not dress in the fine clothes of a gentleman for he knew he would be going to Upper Swandam Lane following the reading.

A hush fell as Charles Dickens walked on stage into the gaslight. Suddenly, a spontaneous crack of applause filled the house. Dickens moved to his personally designed, three-tiered reading desk. Dickens nodded to the audience and after laying his gloves and formal hat on the desk, he picked up a book. Resting his elbow on the highest of the desk's three tiers, he opened the book and began to read selections from *Oliver Twist.*

Dickens' command over his audience amazed de la Rue. The room no longer seemed a collection of individuals but had become one attentive thing, pushed, pulled, driven, frightened, amused, and entertained by the man in the small circle of light.

An hour into the reading Dickens took a ten-minute intermission. De la Rue watched as he closed his book, and moved off-stage. A man emerged from the wings, took Dickens' arm, and led him out of sight. Ten minutes later Dickens returned. This reading would be the murder of Nancy by Bill Sikes. Dickens seemed now to control the very respiration of his audience. There were passages where taking a breath, making a disturbance, however slight, would have been a sacrilegious impossibility. Nancy pleaded for her life. Sikes roared his vengeance and slashed and struck at the helpless woman. The murder, the woman's very blood, seemed visible on stage.

When the passage ended, Dickens held onto his desk with both hands to steady himself. He nodded once in the direction of his audience and stepped away. Again a cannon shot of applause thundered in the hall; and again Dickens needed help. Two men, one quite young, appeared quickly from the wings and took Dickens by the elbows. The way Dickens staggered from the stage shocked de la Rue.

The audience rose and shouted out Dickens' name, but he did not return. De la Rue rose to get a better look at the empty stage. He hoped Dickens would reappear because he could hardly believe his eyes. As those two men escorted Dickens away, he seemed to be an aged, decrepit shadow of the man de la Rue remembered from Genoa. There had been no hint of this when he had seen Dickens for those few minutes at the Athenaeum. He had aged, of course. The long, wavy brown hair had gone gray and thin. The smooth-skinned active face had been battered and creased by those twenty-five years. The eyes, though, had remained sharp and powerful. The man before him tonight, however, ended his performance wasted, weakened, and looked near death.

De la Rue joined the throng heading for the street. He need have no fear of this man, he told himself. The man he saw needed to put every ounce of his strength into the battle to stay alive. But de la Rue wanted to be certain. He knew Dickens would read one last time the following week. Lord Allsgood had already mentioned that many of Dickens' friends in London would attend this final reading, Lord Allsgood among them. He would impose on the good Lord to include him in his party. He wanted another satisfying look at a weakened and failing Dickens.

Content he had spent a profitable evening, Emile de la Rue turned his steps toward Upper Swandam Lane.

Emile de la Rue, less concerned with Dickens after having seen him, continued on with his nightly rounds of dinners, clubs and theatres. On Tuesday, the fifteenth, after an early meal at Simpson's, he, Lord Allsgood, and many other of Dickens' friends made their way to St. James Hall to see Dickens read in public for the final time.

De la Rue was in high spirits. He had not needed to visit Upper Swandam Lane since giving in to the relief he had felt the previous Tuesday night. Hale and well rested, he followed Lord Allsgood to seats only a half-dozen rows from the stage, prepared to enjoy a closer look at an infirm Dickens.

The theatre darkened and Dickens, resplendent as always, geranium in his buttonhole, appeared. The audience cried his name and rose as if hot coals had been slipped onto their chairs. Dickens nodded and looked over the audience. He lifted his hand to quiet them and began. "Marley was dead, to begin with."

Laughter and tears accompanied the reading, and Dickens left the stage for his accustomed ten-minute interval amid a cascade of cheering. When he returned, he began to read the trial from Pickwick. De la Rue, as well as everyone else, was astonished at Dickens inability to pronounce the word "Pickwick." De la Rue swore it came out "Pickswick," "Picnic," and even "Peckswicks."

Dickens either ignored or failed to notice his inability to handle those two syllables and reached the end of the selection. He closed his book and walked off into the waiting arms of his doctor, Frank Beard. The applause commenced and a moment later Dickens reappeared. He quieted the audience and spoke. "I close this episode of my life with feelings of considerable pain. For some fifteen years, in this hall and in many kindred places, I have had the honour of presenting my own cherished ideas before you for your recognition; and, in closely observing your reception of them, have enjoyed an amount of artistic delight and instruction which, perhaps, is given to few men to know." Dickens paused and cast his glance over the now gas-lit auditorium. Abruptly, De la Rue felt Dickens' cold stare on him. Their eyes locked, and Dickens head moved slightly upright. De la Rue stubbornly refused to look away. Of necessity, Dickens lifted his eyes and continued. "In but two short weeks from this time I hope that you may enter, in your own homes, on a new series of readings, at which my assistance will be indispensable..." Dickens reached out and grasped his reading desk with both hands. "...but from these garish lights I vanish now forevermore, with a heartfelt, grateful, respectful, and affectionate farewell."

Dickens kissed his hand to the audience, bowed, and slowly walked off stage into the waiting arms of Frank Beard.

As the theatre exploded with shouts and cheering around him, de la Rue felt a cold chill creeping over him. What had Dickens meant, he would be coming into people's homes? Then de la Rue remembered the placards he had seen lining bookstore windows. A new novel by Mr. Dickens loomed. Why had Dickens chosen the moment after their eyes linked to mention his book? What was in the book? Was Dickens telling him something?

The security de la Rue wrapped himself in when he had seen Dickens' condition now seemed tattered and threadbare. The eerie feeling of the world stepping back from him and dread and anxiety pouring in to fill the empty space swept over him. Only with the greatest of discipline did he keep himself a member of Lord Allsgood's party and not skulk off to the opium dens of Upper Swandam Lane for relief.

Chapter Fifteen

Thursday, March 31. For the fourth time in the past two weeks, Emile de la Rue awoke in the squalid atmosphere of languid debauchery. The moans of the reawakening roused him and for a moment he moaned himself. He knew where he was; he need not open his eyes. Joined to the grim chorus of moans came the sound of shuffling feet as some of the opium smokers decided they had had enough, the allure of a new day sufficient cause for them to reenter the world they had gone there to shun. The ingratiating voice of the Lascar crept into his ear.

"Another pipe, mate?"

De la Rue opened his eyes. The Lascar's face hovered no more than three inches from his own. He closed his eyes and moved his head left and right.

"Time to go then."

De la Rue drew a deep breath and struggled into a sitting position. Half of the cots were still occupied by men nursing their long opium pipes. The old woman who had let him into the den lay on a cot smoking. She noticed his glance and motioned to him to join her. She held her pipe up and smiled a near toothless smile.

De la Rue rose and staggered to the door. The Lascar opened the door, put his hand on de la Rue's shoulder, and firmly guided him into the harsh morning light.

A cold and misty day. De la Rue leaned against the wall near the alley's entrance, opening and closing his eyes to accustom them to the light. His empty stomach growled. He thought back to his mornings with Augusta and the way they would greet each other warmly, lovingly when her health permitted. When her illness left her weak and bedridden, he would take care of her. Now...

He pulled out the cheap pocket watch he had bought to replace the one stolen during a visit to the opium den. The missing watch had been a very expensive one. Now he knew better. Apparently, so did the thieves lurking in the den. The booksellers would open in an hour at nine.

De la Rue made his way back to The Kensington and entered through a side passage. He cleaned himself up, dressed, and breakfasted. In a swirl of dread, he set off for Blandings, the nearest bookseller. Today, the first number of Dickens' new novel went on sale.

Blandings' window displayed the slim, green-covered magazines along with a large photo of Charles Dickens. De la Rue entered, paid his shilling for a copy of *The Mystery of Edwin Drood, Part One*. He rolled it up and put it into his pocket. He could not bring himself to look.

He had seen Dickens four times since his final reading. He knew Dickens would be in town until the end of May when his lease on 5 Hyde Park Place expired. Dickens visited his Wellington Street offices every Thursday and sometimes oftener. He frequently disappeared for days at a time when de la Rue imagined him to be with his actress mistress. De la Rue caught glimpses of Dickens on his trips back and forth between Hyde Park Place and Wellington Street. He knew it was folly to lurk about hoping to get a quick look at Dickens, but he could not help himself.

Dickens and Forster had been together at the Athenaeum on Wednesday of last week, and both men had studiously avoided both him and Lord Allsgood. Again he had been conscious of Forster's cold stare, but he had not caught Dickens looking his way even once. Neither Dickens nor Forster made the slightest attempt at cordiality. He would have much preferred a direct challenge from Dickens to this sly, subtle, subterranean, psychological method of attack, if only so he could know for certain he was *under* attack.

De la Rue turned back toward The Kensington and his sitting room. Seated next to a window, he opened *The Mystery of Edwin Drood.* He ignored the advertisements for self-raising flour and miracle medicines and began to read.

"An ancient English Cathedral Tower?" it began, as John Jasper awoke from his opium dreams. An hour later de la Rue tossed the magazine to the floor and clutched at his stomach where an ache of tension had formed at the very first page of his reading. Opium smoking. An accusation from Dickens? He knew he had never mentioned his habit to Dickens. Had Augusta? Did Dickens know where he spent so many of his nights? No, he could not. Jasper's opium habit could only be a coincidence.

In his story Dickens obviously used details of his time with him and Augusta in Genoa. The portrait of Augusta the Dowd boy commissioned; the gloves he'd showered Augusta with. Those incidents were in the book. Had he mentioned them to Dickens? Maybe he did. He certainly could not remember everything he had told Dickens over the course of their relationship. His Egypt trip was common knowledge, and in the story Dickens has the girl, Rosa Bud, mention

144

Drood's plans to start his career in Egypt.   Both the Dowd boy and Drood engineers?   More coincidence?   And what should he make of the festering love triangle of Jasper secretly infatuated with Rosa Bud, already engaged to Jasper's nephew, Edwin Drood.   Why did Rosa Bud specifically use the word phantoms when another word would have done just as well?

De la Rue scoured his memory, trying to recall what he had told Dickens about himself and Augusta those long years ago, but the memories were faded and cloudy.   No matter where Dickens had gotten his information, *he* seemed to have no problem remembering it all, and now he was using it.   But to what purpose?   Simply to fuel his new story?   Certainly for no other reason.   Dickens could use as many details as he liked.   What would it matter?   No one would know where those details came from.   De la Rue thought of Forster.   How much had Dickens told his friend about Genoa?   And why had Dickens stared so pointedly at him when announcing his new story as he closed his final reading?   How far would Dickens go to fulfill his threat of twenty-five years ago to reveal him to the world as a murderer?

De la Rue balled his hands into fists of frustration.   What the devil was Dickens up to?   Where would it end?   He looked at the magazine now resting upside down on the floor.   Dickens had used a few details from their encounter of twenty-five years ago.   So what?   Nothing in the story so far would bring Emile de la Rue to anyone's mind.   Nothing at all.

De la Rue moved to his bedroom, leaving the slim,

green volume where it lay. He planned to meet Lord Allsgood at six for a visit to the theatre, and he needed to rest. Let Dickens tell his new story. The way Dickens had looked on stage, he would have a difficult time telling a story that would go on for very long anyway.

De la Rue kept a close eye on Dickens. He read in the newspaper about the speech Dickens gave to newsvendors on Tuesday, April 5. Lord Allsgood asked whether he wanted to accompany him to a party Dickens planned to host at Hyde Park Place on Thursday, two days later. De la Rue made his excuses. Better to let sleeping dogs lie, he thought. The following day at the Athenaeum Lord Allsgood reported to him about the party, but imparted only idle and vapid details of the gathering.

De la Rue's heart grew light, and his guilty imaginings melting into memories. When he returned home that evening, though, a plainly wrapped parcel awaited him. He opened it and inside found a copy of the first number of *The Mystery of Edwin Drood*. De la Rue's stomach plummeted, and his heart began to pound. He rummaged over the wrapper and flipped through the pages of the magazine, but he could find no indication of who had sent it. Dickens?

Again he felt the eerie sense of the world backing away from him as dread gushed over and around him. Who else could possibly have sent the magazine? Dickens. Only Dickens. De la Rue knew others in his circle had read the story. Their brief comments acknowledged Dickens to be at the height of his power. Had they bought their copies? Did

Dickens have a list—a courtesy list—of people who received copies at their home? De la Rue shook his head. If Dickens had such a list, *he* would certainly not be on it. Was it Dickens' way of warning him he had better keep an eye on the story? Now he would have to suffer through until the final day of April when the second number would be issued. What would *it* contain?

De la Rue poured himself a brandy and then another, and spent an hour lost in thought. At last, tossing his clothes onto a chair, he went to bed.

Saturday, April 30. Emile de la Rue paced the street in the early morning as he waited for Blandings to open. When it did, de la Rue went inside, browsed a few moments, and then purchased the second number of *The Mystery of Edwin Drood.* He hurried back to The Kensington.

As he read he recognized obvious echoes of Genoa coming down to him through the years. Dickens has Rosa say of Jasper, "He terrifies me. He haunts my thoughts, like a dreadful ghost. I am never safe from him." De la Rue paused and reread the passage. Moments later Rosa says, "He has forced me to understand him, without his saying a word; and he has forced me to keep silence, without his uttering a threat." An argument erupts between Drood and Neville Landless, a third admirer of Rosa, and Dickens has Landless berate Drood by saying, "Your vanity is intolerable, your conceit is beyond endurance; you talk as if you were some rare and precious prize." Dickens' very words to him! Claws of fear racked de la Rue's stomach.

And Rosa—betrothed to one man and being slyly,

underhandedly courted by another, wondering whether to marry at all. Dickens recorded it all, but to what purpose? The question pounded within de la Rue's brain. To what purpose? Dickens would never fulfill his threat by merely coming out and naming him in his story, but if Dickens' intended simply to harass and torment him, he was succeeding. De la Rue knew he could endure and survive Dickens' persecution, though, and that was all he wanted to do. Endure and survive. It would have to see him through.

A week later, the story's second installment arrived anonymously at The Kensington. De la Rue tossed it unopened into the trash and girded himself to await the appearance of the third number of the novel.

Dickens made no public appearances in May. The gossip at the clubs indicated that Dickens health was an issue. He had canceled his attendance at the Queen's ball due to a swollen and painful foot, forcing his daughter to go alone. Dickens still disappeared occasionally to be with his mistress, yet de la Rue knew the writing of his novel went on.

De la Rue was away at Lord Allsgood's country estate at the end of the month, and so could not pick up the June number of *Drood* until late Friday, June 3, when he returned to London. After dinner alone and with a brandy at his elbow, he read it in his sitting room at The Kensington.

Two o'clock in the morning found Emile de la Rue still slumped in his chair, the third number of *The Mystery of Edwin Drood* on the floor next to him. He had not moved since he finished reading. Hours of asking himself the same question—what did Dickens mean by his story—a story of misplaced love, both Neville's and Jasper's for Rosa, causing hatred now and soon, doubtless, a murder. And why this story just after he and Dickens had met again? This episode so teemed with references to Genoa, de la Rue knew coincidence was impossible. De la Rue had read the chapters twice through to be certain he hadn't missed a reference. A caution by Grewgious against an insincere lover, just as Augusta's brother had cautioned her against him. Jasper, planning murder, taking a tour of the cathedral crypts just as he, himself, had taken a tour of the landscape where he knew Charles and Rodney Dowd would hike. But no one knew he had done that, so how could Dickens? A guess? A lucky hit of his imagination? Neville Landless, a brother and convenient suspect and scapegoat when Jasper murders Drood, as seemed surely to be the direction of the story. And the ring, described perfectly, and obviously the important clue that would come back to haunt the murderer. Or so it seemed to de la Rue.

Over and over de la Rue, fruitlessly and against reason, tried to fit Dickens' hints into a pattern of mere coincidence, but it was like trying to cram a right foot into a left boot. It could be done, but not for long and not without ignoring considerable discomfort. From the first scene of the story in the opium den to the underlining of the ruby and diamond ring, there came the steady fall of hints of Genoa like the incessant dripping of rainwater from leaves after the storm has passed. Slow...continuous... maddening.

What would be the outcome? De la Rue roused himself and stood. He refused to believe Dickens would follow through, literally, on his threat to proclaim him a murderer. No, Dickens simply enjoyed tormenting him, and this torment would ultimately prove harmless and of no consequence. De la Rue knew he could endure and survive Dickens' story. If he should encounter Dickens, he would never let on he had even read any of the story. He would rob Dickens of that satisfaction at least.

Anyway, how did Dickens even *know* he'd read any of the story? De la Rue thought of the mysteriously delivered copies of the first two numbers. If they were from Dickens, did Dickens think their delivery enough to ensure he would read them? Perhaps. Since he *was* reading them.

But still, Dickens' threat would not be driven from de la Rue's mind. If only he could be certain, but his only certainty involved another slow, tantalizing wait for the next month's number to come out. De la Rue drank and thought deep into the night. Finally, he threw himself into bed hoping he would see things more clearly after a night's sleep, but images of Genoa and Dickens floated through de la Rue's brandy-driven dreams. Augusta. Charles. Rodney. Rodney Dowd. Fitfully, de la Rue tossed and turned. Rodney Dowd. Edwin Drood. Rodney Dowd. Edwin Drood. De la Rue's eyes sprang open. His breath gushed as if he had rushed up a flight of stairs. My God! Was it possible?

He tossed the covers away and groped for a candle. He lit the candle and staggered to his desk. He put the candle down and grabbed for pen and paper. Rodney Dowd. No, no. There was no "i" so it couldn't be. It couldn't be but it was.

De la Rue stared, unwilling to acknowledge the truth. He now knew for certain what Dickens planned.

Slowly, de la Rue rearranged the letters of Rodney

Dowd's name.

e d w y n d r o o d

Edwin Drood!

De la Rue let his pen tumble to the floor. This was more than building a story on memories of Genoa. This was more than a simple reminder from Dickens that he knew what occurred in Genoa. This was more than an attempt to torment him. Somehow Dickens was writing his story as an act of vengeance on him. For stealing Augusta. For, to Dickens' mind, harming Augusta. For killing the boy. For subduing Dickens in their battle of wills. For sending Dickens home helpless and defeated.

De la Rue crumpled the paper on which he had deciphered Dickens' threat, and a chill thought struck him. How much of the story had Dickens written? How much was left to write? What would he reveal? When would he reveal it? What would happen if Dickens proclaimed him a murderer? Dickens could not possibly make a serious case against him to the police, but to his new circle of acquaintances—the people Lord Allsgood had introduced him to—Dickens voice carried great weight. He would be known as a murderer. He would be detested, exiled. Protest as he might, what would his word be against the word of the most famous Englishman in the land? Then what? Skulk back to Italy in disgrace; back to Genoa, his story known all over Europe? Who would welcome him? How would he live? Where would he find the slightest glimmer of enjoyment or satisfaction? De la Rue cringed at the possibilities. No, he had come to England for a purpose, and he'd achieved his purpose. His life was proceeding exactly as he had planned. He lived in the highest levels of society, and he would not allow Dickens to triumph and strip that away from him.

Dickens' story must end. No more could be written.

De la Rue made up his mind. No more *would* be written.

Chapter Sixteen

Saturday, June 4. Late in the afternoon Emile de la Rue checked into the Imperial Hotel in Rochester. He signed his name Phillipe Visconti. From club talk in London and from common knowledge, he knew certain things already. Dickens' home, Gad's Hill, lay a short distance away along the Rochester High Road, the main route from London to Dover, a road frequented by numerous tramps traveling between cities looking for handouts or even brief employment. He knew Dickens had some short of chalet—a gift from an actor he once assisted and who had become a friend—on his grounds where he wrote during pleasant weather. He knew Dickens lived with his sister-in-law and his one unmarried daughter. He knew Dickens was ill and had returned home. At the moment it was all he knew.

Unfortunately, he could hardly count on Dickens' ill health carrying him off before he completed his accursed *Drood* book. There had to be something in what he already knew or in what he intended to find out which would enable him to make certain *The Mystery of Edwin Drood* never reached completion and quickly.

De la Rue lunched at the hotel and mulled over his possibilities. A look at Dickens' home quickly rose to the top of his list. He returned to his hotel room and changed into clothing he hoped would make him indistinguishable from the tramps commonly seen along the road. He set out.

A brief walk brought him near the house. He loitered

outside the property, eyeing the grand three-story home, complete with rooftop cupola. Bushes ringed the house and a red profusion of geraniums in the garden added brilliant color. De la Rue scanned the garden and saw how Dickens' property continued onto the other side of the road. Through trees and bushes he caught glimpses of the chalet. Ultimately, he noticed the tunnel he had unknowingly walked over and grasped how the tunnel led from Dickens' garden, under the road and onto the property where the chalet stood.

The chalet had two stories, the second story accessible from an outside stairway. A balcony ringed the second floor. From a distance de la Rue inspected the chalet from different angles. The leaf-covered trees, though, prevented a clear view from any angle.

De la Rue continued down the road, taking a long slow look at all of Dickens' property. He walked a half-mile past the house before turning back to take a second close look at the house, grounds, and chalet.

Back in his Rochester hotel room, De la Rue put on more respectable clothing, determined to make the best of the rest of the day by finding out all he could about Dickens' habits at Gad's Hill. He left his room and when he reached the hotel lobby he saw the desk clerk unengaged and approached him.

"Afternoon, sir. Help you?" offered the clerk, a beardless young man with sparse hair on his head and an overly ingratiating way about him.

"Well, yes. I understand Mr. Dickens, the great novelist, lives in the area."

"Oh, yes he does, sir," said the clerk, a bolt of

excitement lighting up his face. "Most everyone who stays here asks after him. We get to see him on occasion. Comes into town to shop with his daughter sometimes, he does."

"I understand he hasn't been well."

With appropriate decorum the clerk let his excitement seep away. "Quite sick at times," and he tapped knowingly on the left side of his chest. "Dr. Steele's been to see him plenty."

"Dr. Steele?"

"Our local doctor. Mr. Dickens has his own doctors in London, of course, but Dr. Steele is always ready to lend a hand."

"Has Mr. Dickens been in town lately? It would be a thrill to have a glimpse of him."

The clerk shook his head. "Been up in London these five months past reading out of his books, though I hear he's returned to Gad's Hill only a few days ago." The clerk pointed in the general direction of Dickens' house. "Lovely house he has. How long will you be here, sir? Like as not you'll get a glimpse of him."

De la Rue smiled and gave a shrug. "A while. Not too long. I've not decided."

The clerk nodded understandingly.

"Well, if you need anything just ask for me, sir. Jemmy Blaine at your service."

"Thank you. Thank you." De la Rue stepped away but stopped and turned back. "Where did you say Dr. Steele had his office?"

"Three blocks over. Albion Street."

De la Rue thanked the clerk and left the hotel.

Albion Street was lined with two-story buildings, shops mostly with rooms to let on the second floor. De la Rue sauntered along the sidewalk until he saw the sign he wanted. Doctor Steele. The sign indicated a second floor office on a corner building. De la Rue went up the outside stairs and put his ear to the door. He heard voices. The good doctor was at work on this Saturday. De la Rue retraced his steps and stood for a moment in front of Dr. Steele's building. Across the street stood the Queen's Tavern, a two-story building of dark brick, the first floor given over to a long, gleaming wooden bar and an assortment of round tables and wooden chairs. De la Rue crossed the street to the tavern and took a seat near a window from which he could watch the doctor's building. He ordered a beer and sipped it, plotting a way to meet this Dr. Steele.

Just past five o'clock the doctor's door at the top of the stairs opened. An older, white-haired man dressed in a dull black suit emerged. The man inserted a key into the lock and fussed with it a moment. He took the key out and held it up to the light. He put the key back into his pocket and reached into his small black bag for another key. He inserted this second key in the door. He removed it, tested the knob, and seemed satisfied with his work. The key, though, slipped out of his hand and dropped onto the landing. Making a stuttery circle with his feet, he looked for the key. He took off his derby hat and scratched his head.

De la Rue bustled out the door of the tavern and crossed the street. He stopped near the bottom of the Doctor's stairs. Up on the landing the Doctor made clumsy circles, shuffling every which way looking for the key. De la

Rue looked behind the stairs and saw a key lying on the ground under the landing. He went and picked it up, looking up when he rose, key in hand. The key had fallen through one of the spaces between the planks of the landing.

De la Rue stepped out where the Doctor could see him,

"Excuse me. Doctor Steele?"

Doctor Steele looked toward the sky.

"No, down here, sir."

The Doctor spun around again and leaned his head over the rail of the landing, his hat nearly coming off in the process.

"Are you looking for a key, Doctor?" De la Rue held the key above his head.

"A key? Is that my key? How..." The Doctor inspected the floor of the landing. He gave a short laugh. "Sometimes I think if my head wasn't attached to my neck, I'd misplace *it*. Fell through, did it?"

"I couldn't help but notice your dilemma," de la Rue explained.

Doctor Steele made his way down the stairs, holding tightly to the rail. When he reached the ground, he took the key and put it into his black bag. The doctor was a short, stooped man who looked to be somewhat past de la Rue's age. He wore thick glasses and had a bushy white mustache. He had somehow scuffed the coloring from the toe of his right shoe.

"Thank you, sir," said the Doctor. "Saturdays are always long days. Start early and usually have to skip lunch. Mrs. Casey," he nodded, tipping his hat to a matronly woman passing by.

"Your wife will no doubt have a wonderful dinner awaiting you?"

"Wife! No, sir. No wife. Never had, never will." He pointed across the street. "The Queen's Tavern is good enough for me."

"Ah, just where I was heading. I'm new here in the city and also without a wife." De la Rue smiled agreeably. "Would you be opposed to my buying you a drink?"

"Opposed? Certainly not, sir, but you have the advantage of me. You are...?"

"Phillipe Visconti. From Switzerland, retired. Sold all my properties and have come to England. I'm staying at the Imperial at the moment."

"Come to England, have you. Excellent choice. Excellent. Finest country on Earth. Come, let's go and have that drink."

The two men walked to the curbside and waited as a string of carriages passed by. They gingerly made their way through the debris of the street and crossed over to the Queen's Tavern. De la Rue followed the doctor toward a small table in the back of the room.

"My usual place in the scheme of things," the doctor explained. "I dine here most evenings."

When they sat, the doctor patted his pockets.

"Have you lost something else?" de la Rue asked, planting a smile on his face.

"My glasses. Did I leave them in the office?"

De la Rue quietly sighed and touched himself on the forehead. "Up here."

The doctor's hand sprang to his brow where his glasses perched. He laughed. "If my head wasn't attached..." The doctor's chuckling drowned out the rest of the sentence.

De la Rue engaged the doctor in idle chatter while the waiter drew their beers and delivered them to the table. When the doctor had drained two-thirds of his glass, de la Rue indicated to the waiter they needed refills. He addressed the doctor. "I hear your famous novelist has returned to his home. Mr. Dickens."

Doctor Steele nodded, running his tongue over his mustache looking for beer foam. "Yes. Been here since Friday when I sent down his laudanum."

"Laudanum?" Perhaps those opium scenes in Dickens' novel came from personal experience, thought de la Rue.

Steele drew himself up and assumed a gravitas which gave de la Rue hope the good doctor would be willing to display his importance—his *self*-importance—in town.

"Yes. The poor man hasn't been well. His London doctors have written..." He cleared his throat. "...and requested I keep a close eye on him. Let them know if they're needed."

"Why does he need laudanum?"

"Foot. Terrible pain. Sleeping is difficult."

The waiter placed two more pints of beer on the table. Seeing this, the doctor raised his first glass to his lips and emptied it. He searched his mustache again before smiling his gratitude at de la Rue.

De la Rue gestured his thanks were unnecessary.

"But I doubt you've come to Rochester to hear about

Mr. Dickens' foot," the doctor chuckled.

"No, of course not, but oddly, I have a sister—she's back in Switzerland—who suffers from complaints similar to Mr. Dickens. The doctors there..." He shrugged to indicate their hopelessness.

"What ails your sister?" The doctor took a long pull from his new beer.

De la Rue searched his memory for the club talk he had heard regarding Dickens.

"One side of her body seems weaker than the other. Her right hand and right foot sometimes refuse to obey her commands."

The doctor nodded knowingly.

"The doctors say her heart is the cause of the weakness. They give her medicines, but..." De la Rue shrugged.

"Digitalis, no doubt."

"Digitalis?"

"Standard for a weak heart."

"Well, they must not give her enough. Her complaints persist."

The doctor chuckled. "No, don't want to give too much. Digitalis is like..." He paused to chuckle again. "...female companionship. A little goes a long way, and too much can kill you." The doctor laughed aloud, quite pleased with his jest.

De la Rue showed appreciation for the doctor's wit and said, "I will write her to see if this...what did you call it?"

"Digitalis. Odd story of its discovery." The doctor paused to see whether de la Rue would allow him to tell it.

160

De la Rue, intent on staying in the doctor's good graces, invited the digression.

"How so?"

"Why in, I think 1775 or so, a Scottish doctor name of Withering, William Withering, lived in Staffordshire. Couldn't cure one of his patients from the effects of a weak heart. Patient came back cured. Doctor wanted to know how. From a potion given him by a gypsy said the patient. Withering tracked down the gypsy and learned the formula. The ingredient in the potion that affected the cure was digitalis extract from the leaves of the purple foxglove. Doctors have been using it ever since."

"That's amazing," said de la Rue. "How does it work?"

"I know its effects. Just how the effects come about..." The doctor shrugged.

"Go on."

"Strengthens the heart. Steadies the heart. Makes the weak heart more powerful."

"Why would too much be a danger, then? Seems to me the stronger the heart the better."

The doctor emptied his mug and shook his head. "The heart could be overpowered, being weak to begin with. Or a weakness in the system elsewhere could be exacerbated and cause apoplexy."

"Strange how something that saves can also destroy."

"Not unlike good beer," the doctor chuckled.

De la Rue echoed the doctor's laughter again and called for two more mugs while he thought over what the doctor had told him. Ending his brief reverie, he said,

"Dinner, doctor. You must allow me to buy dinner."

The doctor sputtered a demurral claiming over-generosity on the part of his new friend, but de la Rue insisted and the men dined. For the remainder of their evening together, de la Rue let the doctor ramble on at his whim. He tried again later to engage the doctor in conversation regarding Dickens' condition and his own fictional Swiss sister, but apparently the doctor had said all he cared to say on the topic. Just after eight o'clock, the men separated, the doctor declaring de la Rue one of the finest men he had ever met and leaving him with the benediction that he make Rochester his permanent home.

Sunday, June 5. De la Rue walked the streets of Rochester trying to invent other ways of learning the habits of Dickens' Gad's Hill life but found scant opportunity. In mid-afternoon he dressed himself as a tramp again and sauntered along the high road past Gad's Hill. There were people scattered on the lawn in front of Dickens' home, so de la Rue pulled his hat down over his brow and did not stop. Again he walked a half-mile or so past the house and turned around. On his return trip de la Rue caught a glimpse of Dickens himself sitting on a chair, his guests milling about him. He returned to his hotel to consider.

Over a lonely dinner and a bottle of wine he decided to rise early the next day and position himself near enough Gad's Hill to learn what went on in the morning. It would be easy enough. If Dickens rarely left Gad's Hill, which seemed to be the case, then de la Rue would have to find a way to go to him. Preventing the completion of the *Drood* novel was paramount, but how in heaven's name could he accomplish it? It would not be easy to dispose of Mr. Charles Dickens before he did irreparable harm. Not easy; but yet, de la Rue trusted, not impossible.

Chapter Seventeen

If only Dickens' heart would experience its inevitable failure and take this burden from him. If only he had gone somewhere other than England to settle. If only Dickens had never visited Genoa. Emile de la Rue nursed these thoughts as he crouched in a field off the Rochester High Road near Gad's Hill as a new day dawned. Before him across the road lay Dickens' house and garden. To his left, through the trees stood the chalet. It was very early Monday morning and de la Rue wanted this onerous, murderous chore completed by week's end—completed, of course, in a manner that cast no suspicion his way. Completed even in a manner that cast no suspicion at all. An accident. Anything without intentionality emblazoned on it: a fall down the stairs of the chalet; a tumble over the second floor balcony railing; a fall in the garden, head fatally striking rock. If Dickens did smoke opium and did frequent a Rochester smoking den, his death could easily be disguised as a crime occasioned by place. As de la Rue considered, he toyed with a small pair of binoculars around his neck. He knew, though, that Dickens' use of laudanum did not necessarily mean he included opium in his habits. Plus, how would a man of his renown make his way unknown into such a den? De la Rue cast the crime in an opium den possibility aside.

He glanced at his watch. Just past 7 o'clock and still no activity on Dickens' property. De la Rue's mind found Augusta. The genuine hope he had originally felt when

Dickens tamed her wildest attacks now angered him. The possibility he himself had caused Augusta's attacks angered him. The audacity of Dickens treating him in this disrespectful, belligerent, month-by-month taunting fashion angered him. The possibility of his having to leave England detested by everyone who mattered to him angered him. This had to be the week he removed the threat of Dickens from his life.

One servant girl, then two, appeared on the lawn, coming from the back of the grand house. De la Rue put his binoculars to use. The servants talked. One laughed. The one who laughed held a large jug with both hands in a way that indicated its fullness, probably of water, de la Rue thought. The other girl carried a stack of blue papers and what looked like pen and ink. De la Rue followed their advance across the garden. When they approached the tunnel, he lost sight of them. De la Rue shifted his position and waited for them to reemerge. From where he hid, he could see one side of the chalet through the trees, the side with the stairs to the second floor. The two servant girls reappeared, climbed the stairs, and entered the chalet. Try as he might, the spread of green leaves prevented his seeing inside the room. He waited.

Two minutes later the girls exited. The girl now held the jug by its neck and casually with one hand. The other girl's hands were empty. They retraced their path to the back of the house.

On the spur of the moment de la Rue rushed in a crouch toward the chalet. Knowing the tunnel, the road, and the riot of greenery hid a view of the chalet from the main house, he climbed the stairs quickly and ducked into the second floor room. He saw the blue papers on a desk against the far window. The pens and ink lay next to the papers. An ornately etched carafe filled with water stood on the corner of the desk along with two overturned glasses. He quickly left the room and looked over the stairs and the balcony. He descended and rapidly returned to his hiding place.

Fifteen minutes later Dickens appeared at his front door. He emerged onto the lawn and looked around. He walked through the garden and toward the rear of the house. He reappeared, having circled the house, and went back inside.

De la Rue waited.

Dickens came back out of the house just before nine and headed through the garden toward the chalet. De la Rue watched him climb the stairs, noticing with a small degree of satisfaction how Dickens clasped the handrail and his brief pause midway up the stairs. He went inside and de la Rue knew more of the accursed novel would be produced that morning.

De la Rue found his way back onto the road and returned to Rochester. He breakfasted and walked the city until noon. He decided to return Gad's Hill.

De la Rue waited for a lull in the traffic along the road and when one occurred, he went back into hiding. He could not tell whether Dickens was still in the chalet or not. A gardener puttered among the geraniums near the main house. Birdsong punctuated the quiet. Carriages and foot traffic moved steadily but sporadically along the high road.

At one-thirty Dickens came carefully down the stairs

of the chalet. De la Rue watched him closely. Though he had no need to pause on the downward trip, the faltering man held tightly to the banister. When Dickens reached the ground, he smoothed his hair with both hands and seemed to gather himself for the trip back through the tunnel and across the garden. Moments later Dickens disappeared inside his home.

De la Rue knew that would end Dickens' writing for the day. He might later be able to catch Dickens going for a walk, but from the way Dickens had climbed the stairs, it seemed very unlikely he would walk far or even walk alone if he walked at all. De la Rue gave up his post and returned to Rochester. He went to the Goose Quill, a tavern down the street from the Imperial Hotel, and ordered lunch and a beer. He had to make up his mind immediately how to deal with Dickens.

Back in his hotel room three hours later, de la Rue had narrowed his possibilities to two; either an accident or somehow giving Dickens an overdose of laudanum or digitalis, the heart medicine Dr. Steele mentioned. Neither option was the obvious one. For an accident to occur, he would have to face Dickens, perhaps even grapple with him, push him down the chalet stairs or over the balcony; crash his head in with a rock—a daunting proposition to say the least. To administer medicine he would have to get into Dickens' home and dose him—even more daunting. Unless...

If he presumed Dickens followed the same regimen daily, the carafe of water sat unattended on his desk for an hour or more in the morning before he arrived at the chalet. If only he could dose the water and be nowhere near when Dickens fell ill from its effects…but he knew nothing about this digitalis. He thought of Upper Swandom Lane.

He would have no problem getting whatever kind of drug he needed and instructions on how to use it in the hovels and byways of Upper Swandom Lane, and he could be up to London and back before midnight. If the trip gave him the information and the medicine he needed, he could dose Dickens' water tomorrow morning. If he failed in that he would have no alternative but to arrange for Dickens to fall prey to an accident.

De la Rue dressed right away and headed for the train station.

Early next morning, dressed again as a tramp, de la Rue crouched in the bushes near Gad's Hill. Only one servant girl holding a jug made the morning trip to the chalet. De la Rue navigated the stairs of the chalet the moment the servant girl disappeared inside the big house. He had learned what he needed to know in London and after handing over a considerable amount of money had procured four vials of the heart drug, each vial sufficient, he was told, to induce paroxysm in a man with a weak heart—if a sufficient dose of the vial—at least half—were ingested.

He took the first vial from his pocket, uncapped it, and after pouring the contents into the carafe of water, he hurried down the stairs and back into hiding. He did not intend to wait around and watch the slow progress of his scheme unfold. There would be no point. If Dickens fell ill, it would doubtless be Dr. Steele who would be the first one summoned. It would be much easier and far less dangerous to keep a watch on the doctor. Giving himself adequate time to calm down—for his own heart had been racing—he sat on the ground, hidden, imagining the outcome: Dickens' collapse; the concern, even panic of his housemates; the call for the doctor, and the tragic result. Feeling more hopeful than he had felt since he started on his deadly excursion, de la Rue made his way back to Rochester.

After a day unmitigated by any slackening of his tense anticipation, de la Rue left his hotel room and walked the few blocks to the Queen's Tavern. It was just past six o'clock and the sun shone brightly. He settled himself at the bar and waited, glancing frequently through the front window of the tavern at the doctor's office. Half an hour later a woman with a little boy in tow came down the doctor's stairs. De la Rue watched them go up the street. Ten minutes later Doctor Steele fumbled about on his landing, locking his office door. De la Rue gripped the edge of the bar as he followed the doctor's halting progress down the stairs and across the street toward him. When the doctor entered the tavern, de la Rue beckoned the man.

"Doctor Steele, I noticed you through the window crossing the street."

"Ah, Mr. Visconti. How are you? How are you?" The doctor glanced toward his usual table. "Have you dined?"

De la Rue shook his head. "To tell you the truth, I hoped you might show up here. I haven't had a decent conversation with a living soul since we two dined together."

"Join me then, please. Today was a good day. Lots of sickness." He laughed softly. "Lots of fees. Dinner shall be my treat tonight."

De la Rue politely protested, but the doctor insisted. "I am in your debt for Saturday night. Come." The doctor led him toward his table. "Of course, we will each pay as we go if we continue to have these pleasant dinners, but tonight, I insist you be my guest."

They sat and ordered.

Finally, de la Rue asked, "So were you called away today? Emergencies rife throughout the metropolis?"

"No, a quiet day as far as that goes, but sixteen patients today, sixteen—all in the office. Seems to be some kind of fever going about among our young. Bless their little hearts." The doctor bubbled with happiness over his good fortune.

De la Rue's enthusiasm for the doctor's company dissipated rapidly with this report, but he had no choice but to sit through the dinner and listen to the doctor talk about his day's work. The doctor did ask whether de la Rue had written to his sick sister in Switzerland. De la Rue said he had, but that was the closest the conversation came to heart degeneration, digitalis, and Dickens. Just after nine o'clock the two men separated.

Wednesday, June 8. Back in hiding de la Rue watched the servant girl carry her jug of water into the chalet but noticed something he had not seen before. The girl emerged onto the balcony and emptied the glass carafe over the railing. She went back inside and a moment later went down the stairs, the empty jug dangling from her hand.

Dickens had not drunk the water. De la Rue's stomach clenched into a mass of fear. He did not drink the water. How could his plan work? Would he ultimately be forced to meet Dickens head on? De la Rue hurried to the stairs and again emptied a vile of digitalis into the newly filled water carafe. He returned immediately to Rochester, but could not stand the waiting, the uncertainty. By noon he had returned to his lair near Gad's Hill. At one, Dickens emerged from the chalet and walked back to the main house. De la Rue's heart began to pound. He had to go and see immediately whether Dickens had drunk the dosed water. He speedily made his way to the chalet steps and glanced toward the house, but all de la Rue could see from the bottom of the stairs were the green and brown of the trees and bushes and the blue of the sky. He raced up the steps and entered the second floor. The carafe remained full, the glasses still turned upside down.

De la Rue clenched his fists in frustration and hurried back down the stairs. He found his way to the high road and began walking. Two days. Two failures. At least he had no need to dine with that miserable doctor tonight. Two vials left. One of them must do its work. One must! Otherwise, there would need to be a face-to-face confrontation with Dickens. Come what may, though, he told himself, the end of this week would bring with it an end to his untenable situation.

All through the long day his ardent desire to spend the night in opium dreams devoured Emile de la Rue. He knew, though, if he surrendered to his urge he would have no chance to be abroad before dawn, hiding in the bushes near Gad's Hill and trying once again to poison Dickens. He settled instead for purchasing a small bottle of brandy and consumed it in his hotel room. When he drained the bottle dry, de la Rue went to sleep.

As we know, Charles Dickens altered his writing schedule this next to last day of his life. He lunched and smoked a cigar afterwards. Then he returned to the chalet to write some more, and sometime during the afternoon, he needed to quench his thirst. At approximately five o'clock, after he returned to the main house, he felt ill. At six o'clock he collapsed.

Thursday, June 9. Morning found Emile de la Rue in his accustomed hiding place somewhat the worse for wear. The previous night's brandy along with his early rising made him groggy. As the new day brightened, de la Rue was surprised to see a number of gigs in front of Dickens' house. He could hear the horses' whinnies every once in a while. Seven o'clock and then seven-thirty came and went but no servant girl took a jug of water to the chalet. Eight o'clock passed. A woman emerged from the house and stepped onto the broad lawn between the house and the road. De la Rue put his binoculars to his eyes. The woman was crying.

Crying! She paced the lawn for a few moments and then, wiping her eyes with the loose cloth of her long skirt, she went back inside.

De la Rue felt hope. From the pounding of his heart to the vivid visions of his imagination he felt hope! Could Dickens have succumbed to his ailments on his own? He turned first toward the chalet and then back toward the house. Both structures sat silent and full of secrets in the morning sun. As de la Rue weighed his next step, another gig entered the grounds of Gad's Hill. He put his binoculars to his eyes again. A man in a dark suit stepped out of it. The man carried a small bag in his right hand, a bag too small to contain clothing. A doctor! The man could only be a doctor! Steele? No, a stranger. De la Rue watched the front door open, and the man hurried inside.

De la Rue thought of the dosed carafe of water. Dickens had not drunk any yesterday morning. Had heaven granted him a stroke of impossible good luck? Was the carafe still full? Would it be better to dispose of the poisoned water? He moved toward the chalet. He hurried up the stairs and ducked inside. Only an inch of water remained in the carafe, and one of the drinking glasses stood right side up! He looked over Dickens' desk. A pen had lain in the center of the desk yesterday next to the neat pile of fresh blue paper, but the pen was missing and the stack of blue paper disarranged! *And there remained only an inch of water in the carafe!* No servant had come to empty the carafe. De la Rue knew that for a certainty. Dickens must have returned to the chalet after lunch the day before! He had drunk the water! There could be no other explanation. But de la Rue needed to know more; he needed to be sure. Doctor Steele. He would go back Rochester and find Dr. Steele.

De la Rue stood on the landing and pounded on Dr. Steele's locked door. He got no answer. He looked to the Queen's Tavern and hurried down the stairs and crossed the street. The tavern did not open until noon. De la Rue calmed himself and began to walk. No reason to hurry, he told himself. The doctor might be at Gad's Hill. Or he might be at his home—de la Rue cursed himself for not having the foresight to inquire where the doctor lived—after being out all night. Who knew what time Dickens had been stricken?

At noon de la Rue returned to the Queen's Tavern and ordered lunch. The gossip had already reached the city. Have you heard, the waiter asked him? Heard what? Mr. Dickens has had an attack. There is little hope of recovery. When was the attack? The previous night the answer came back.

De la Rue watched as people came into the tavern and spoke together. He moved to the bar to eavesdrop. The talk was all Dickens. No hope of recovery. Doctors arrived from London. Very serious. Both daughters and mistress in attendance. No hope of recovery. No hope of recovery.

De la Rue left the tavern and returned to his room. He threw himself on his bed and replayed the conversations he had overheard. He was so close to safety. Sometime soon he would hear the words he needed to hear. Dickens was dead. Dead. Dead.

Just after six o'clock de la Rue returned to the Queen's

Tavern. He learned that Doctor Steele had not put in an appearance all day. De la Rue sat at the bar and nursed a beer. The bar patrons had heard no news about Dickens' condition other than "no hope of recovery." How lovely the phrase sounded in de la Rue's ears, but where the devil was the doctor? Seven o'clock passed. Then eight.

Finally, at ten minutes past eight, Doctor Steele walked into the tavern. He looked very weary and more disheveled than ever. He carried his hat in his hand. The patrons, nearly as one, turned his way. He saw their stares and shook his head. In a soft voice audible to everyone in the hushed room he said, "Mr. Dickens has died. Two hours since. Our great man is gone."

After a moment of stunned quiet, people began to discuss the news. Steele noticed de la Rue, walked over, and took a seat next to him.

"It is true?" asked de la Rue, trying his best to portray a moroseness he did not feel.

Steele nodded. He had been called just after six the day before and had stayed for hours by Dickens' side. The cause? A rupture of a vessel in the brain. Not unexpected, the doctor muttered sagely. When the first of the two expected London doctors arrived late at night, he had gone home. At five o'clock he had returned to see whether he could be helpful. Dickens died at just past six. He had stayed a brief while out of respect and then left. The London doctors would handle the details.

Doctor Steele concluded, "I won't be dining tonight. Just not up to it. I'll have something in my rooms. Perhaps tomorrow night I'll see you here, Mr. Visconti?"

De la Rue said he would look forward to it.

The next morning, however, Emile de la Rue caught an early train up to London.

Chapter Eighteen

Emile de la Rue quietly reinserted himself into the club life of London. Dickens' death was on everyone's lips, and de la Rue never tired of hearing the details. On the Wednesday following, June 15, he along with Lord Allsgood and a number of others went to Westminster Abbey and joined the line of mourners who slowly walked past Dickens' open grave. Bouquets had been tossed everywhere, filling the grave opening and pouring out onto the floor. Through Thursday dusk the grave remained open for public visitation. When the visitations ceased, it was all over.

Friday, June 17. Emile de la Rue paid a visit to the offices of Chapman and Hall. There, in response to his question, a clerk, eager to display an inside knowledge of the great man's legacy, told de la Rue that Chapman and Hall had two more episodes of *The Mystery of Edwin Drood* in hand and Dickens was working on a third when he died, and there would certainly be two more monthly numbers, possibly three.

This caused de la Rue concern. What would these numbers say about him? Did he dare stay around London to find out?

He had been considering a return to Italy for a brief spell, and now seemed the wisest time to make the trip. Therefore, he put it about that he planned a two or three month sojourn abroad, and on the final day of June, he bought the fourth number of Dickens' novel and read it on the boat-train to Southhampton. When he finished reading, he knew his decision to leave England for a while was sound. In number four the murder took place. The three men were brought together. The murderer, the victim and a brother, someone the murderer could shift the blame to. De la Rue felt the familiar flood of fear sweep over him. Dickens is dead now, he told himself. The story will not go on much longer.

De la Rue closed his eyes and leaned his head back against the train seat. He had not realized how much this battle with Dickens had affected him. He had not felt well since his return from Rochester, and he did not feel well now. He'd opted to sail back to Italy rather than take trains in hope the sea air would restore him.

He had arranged for the final two numbers of *Drood* to be sent to him in Genoa, where he would be staying. After he read and digested the final number he would decide whether he could safely return to London. He knew Dickens had planned twelve numbers for the book, and so had scarcely finished half of it. There should be nothing, he told himself, to keep him away from England when the final words of the book should reach the public eye. He alone understood what Dickens planned to disclose with his damnable story. He alone and no one else.

De la Rue boarded his ship, which set sail with the tide. In his diary he recorded fits of nausea and a general lassitude. Early in the morning in his bed on the second day out, Emile de la Rue died of a heart attack. His body continued on to Genoa for burial, where an older brother

178

dealt with his possessions. Some possessions were put to use; some discarded; some put into storage. Among the things stored away was a diary, relegated to the bottom of a box full of papers that might or might not be needed at some future time. They never were needed and lay in a dusty attic for over a century.

And so it was that Emile de la Rue took from Charles Dickens whatever time he had left on earth. How much time? There is no guessing, but I do know thousands of Dickens' readers would gladly take a minute off their own lives—and I more than that—and give all those minutes retroactively to Dickens; others to allow him to complete the great mystery story he left behind; I so Dickens could have exposed Emile de la Rue for a cowardly murderer.

This is but fancy, though. What is not fancy, however, is that Emile de la Rue cut short Charles Dickens' life by untold days, weeks, months, perhaps even years, and while the mystery of Edwin Drood will forever remain unsolved, the mystery of Charles Dickens' death has been answered.

The End

APPENDIX

Mesmerism

Mesmerism can be defined as the ability to so affect a person's consciousness as to put that person into a trance-like state. The word derives from a German physician by the name of Franz Anton Mesmer (1734-1815). Mesmer theorized that people's health and well-being were influenced by the effect of the gravitational pull of the planets on an unidentifiable fluid inside the human body. He believed a magnetic force could affect this mysterious bodily fluid and for a time affected his cures using large metal magnets. The medical profession thought this a bit gimmicky, and so Mesmer decided that simply staring into the person's eyes would do the trick. He developed techniques which put people into a trance-like state during which the bodily fluids could be forced back into their proper equilibrium thereby bringing about a cure.

Many patients applauded Mesmer's treatments, professing to be cured of their symptoms. The medical profession proved not as laudatory. Forced to leave Vienna, Mesmer settled in Paris in 1778 and found numerous patients wishing to be "mesmerised." Both Mozart and Marie Antoinette were patients of Mesmer,[1] and for a time Mesmer—and mesmerism—was a sensation.

---

[1] The first production of a Mozart opera debuted in Mesmer's garden, and Mozart included a scene on mesmerism in his opera Cosi fan tutte.

But history repeated itself and the medical profession in France did not take kindly to replacing bleeding with the application of mesmeric touches and stares. King Louis XVI appointed a commission to take a scientific look into Mesmer's claims. The commission, which included Benjamin Franklin and Dr. Joseph Guillotine, found no scientific basis for Mesmer's claims.[2]   Thoroughly discredited he went quietly back to Switzerland to spend the rest of his life and died there in 1815. The mesmerism movement he had begun, however, went on without him. Which leads us to England's Dr. John Elliotson (1791-1868).

Dr. Elliotson became acquainted with the principles of mesmerism in the 1830's when Baron du Potet, a French mesmerist, visited London. Elliotson, already a leading proponent of one Victorian pseudo-science, phrenology—the belief that facial features are a clue to character and the shape of the head an indication of intelligence—was open to the claims of mesmerism.

Elliotson was a serious physician of note, "one of the most brilliant men in the history of English medicine" according to one medical historian.[3]

---

[2]   Mesmer failed a test in which he hoped that a mesmerized twelve-year-old boy would be able to select a "magnetized" tree from among many trees.

[3]   Elliotson's mainstream credentials are impressive: Professor of the Practice of Medicine in London University from 1831 until 1838; President of the Royal Medical and Surgical Society; a founder of the University College Hospital in London. He also introduced the stethoscope to

On the pseudo-scientific side, however, Elliotson reported that using mesmerism, he himself had achieved many successes involving the cure of facial tics—the exact ailment which Dickens would undertake to cure with Madame de la Rue—and subsequently founded the Mesmeric Hospital in London in 1846.[4]

Dr. Elliotson gave public demonstrations of mesmerism at London University, four of which Dickens is known to have attended, and it is doubtless at one of these lectures that Dickens met Dr. Elliotson. Dickens soon made him his trusted family doctor and steady dinner companion. It is from Dr. Elliotson Dickens learned the principals of mesmerism and the ability to mesmerize.[5]

There are numerous records of Dickens mesmerizing both friends and family. To cite one instance, it is

---

medicine.

[4]   Elliotson was also a founding member of the Phrenological Society, established in 1823. In 1843 he founded *The Zoist: A Journal of Cerebral Physiology and Mesmerism,* which from April 1843, until December 31, 1855, published numerous articles detailing the medical successes of mesmerism, including two successful amputations of the penis using mesmerism as an anesthetic.

[5]   A final note on Dr. Elliotson's prominence in literary Victorian England—Thackeray uses his name in a simile in the first few lines of Chapter twenty-three of *Vanity Fair*, no doubt assuming his name would be instantly recognizable, and he also dedicated his novel, *Pendennis,* to the good doctor for saving his life with his unique procedures.

documented that in 1849 John Leech, an illustrator Dickens used, was knocked over by a wave while sporting in the surf and received a concussion. When leeches applied to his temples did not result in any improvement, Dickens offered to mesmerize him. Leech accepted his offer and recovered.[6]

Suffice it to say that mesmerism was ingrained in the popular culture of Dickens' day and heartily embraced by Dickens himself. In Genoa in 1844, Dickens would call upon the powers of mesmerism to cure a facial tic that tormented Augusta de la Rue, and the chain of events leading to the murder of Charles Dickens would be set in motion.

---

[6] Furthermore, in a letter written from America in May 1842 Dickens crows that Elliotson would be interested to know that "in six minutes, I magnetized her (Catherine, Dickens' wife) into hysterics, and then into a magnetic sleep. I tried again next night, and she fell into the slumber in little more than two minutes."

Also from MX Publishing

Four books on Sir Arthur Conan Doyle by Alistair Duncan including a an overview of all the stories (**Eliminate The Impossible**), a London guide (**Close to Holmes**), the winner of the Howlett Award 2011 (**The Norwood Author**) and the book on Undershaw (**An Entirely New Country**).

Short fiction collections from Tony Reynolds (**Lost Stories of Sherlock Holmes**), Gerard Kelly (**The Outstanding Mysteries of Sherlock Holmes**) and Bertram Fletcher Robinson (**Aside Arthur Conan Doyle**).

www.mxpublishing.com

Also From MX Publishing

 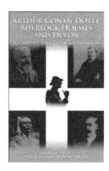 

A biography (**In Search of Dr Watson**), a travel guide (**Sherlock Holmes and Devon**), a novel where Sherlock Holmes battles The Phantom (**Rendezvous at The Populaire**), a novel featuring Dr. Watson (**Watson's Afghan Adventure**), a fantasy novel (**Shadowfall**) and an intriguing collection of papers from The Hound (**The Official Papers Into The Matter Known as The Hound of The Baskervilles**).

www.mxpublishing.com

Also From MX Publishing

Two 'Female Sherlock Holmes' novels (**The Sign of Fear and A Study In Crimson**) the definitive **A Chronology of Sir Arthur Conan Doyle**, a biography of **Bertram Fletcher Robinson**, reprint of the novel **Wheels of Anarchy** and the 4 'Lost Playlets of P.G.Wodehouse (**Bobbles and Plum**).

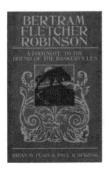  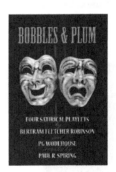

www.mxpublishing.com

Also From MX Publishing

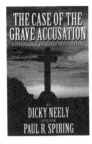

The Case of The Grave Accusation

The creator of Sherlock Holmes has been accused of murder. Only Holmes and Watson can stop the destruction of the Holmes legacy.

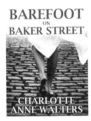

Barefoot on Baker Street

Epic novel of the life of a Victorian workhouse orphan featuring Sherlock Holmes and Moriarty.

Case of Witchcraft

A tale of witchcraft in the Northern Isles, in which long-concealed secrets are revealed -- including some that concern the Great Detective himself!

Also From MX Publishing

The Affair In Transylvania

Holmes and Watson tackle Dracula
in deepest Transylvania in this
stunning adaptation by film director
Gerry O'Hara

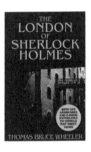

The London of Sherlock Holmes

400 locations including GPS co-
ordinates that enable Google Street
view of the locations around
London in all the Homes stories

I Will Find The Answer

Sequel to Rendezvous At The
Populaire, Holmes and Watson tackle
Dr.Jekyll.

www.mxpublishing.com

Also From MX Publishing

The Case of The Russian Chessboard

Short novel covering the dark world of Russian espionage sees Holmes and Watson on the world stage facing dark and complex enemies.

An Entirely New Country

Covers Arthur Conan Doyle's years at Undershaw where he wrote Hound of The Baskervilles. Foreword by Mark Gatiss (BBC's Sherlock).

Shadowblood

Sequel to Shadowfall, Holmes and Watson tackle blood magic, the vilest form of sorcery.

www.mxpublishing.com

Also From MX Publishing

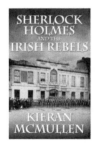

Sherlock Holmes and The Irish Rebels

It is early 1916 and the world is at war.
Sherlock Holmes is well into his spy
persona as Altamont.

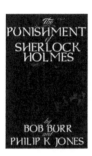

The Punishment of Sherlock Holmes

"deliberately and successfully funny"

The Sherlock Holmes Society of
London

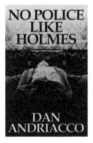

No Police Like Holmes

It's a Sherlock Holmes symposium,
and murder is involved. The first case
for Sebastian McCabe.

www.mxpublishing.com

Also From MX Publishing

In The Night, In The Dark

Winner of the Dracula Society Award
– a collection of supernatural ghost
stories from the editor of the Sherlock
Holmes Society of London journal.

Sherlock Holmes and
The Lyme Regis Horror

Fully updated 2nd edition of this
bestselling Holmes story set in Dorset.

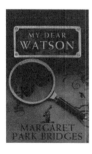

My Dear Watson

Winner of the Suntory Mystery Award
for fiction and translated from the
original Japanese. Holmes greatest
secret is revealed – Sherlock Holmes is
a woman.

www.mxpublishing.com

Also From MX Publishing

Mark of The Baskerville Hound

100 years on and a New York policeman faces a similar terror to the great detective.

A Professor Reflects On Sherlock Holmes

A wonderful collection of essays and scripts and writings on Sherlock Holmes.

Sherlock Holmes On The Air

A collection of Sherlock Holmes radio scripts with detailed notes on Canonical references.

www.mxpublishing.com

Also From MX Publishing

Sherlock Holmes Whos Who

All the characters from the entire canon catalogued and profiled.

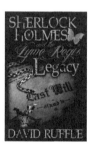

Sherlock Holmes and The Lyme Regis Legacy

Sequel to the Lyme Regis Horror and Holmes and Watson are once again embroiled in murder in Dorset.

Sherlock Holmes and The Discarded Cigarette

London 1895. A well known author, a theoretical invention made real and the perfect crime.

www.mxpublishing.com

Also From MX Publishing

Sherlock Holmes and The Whitechapel
Vampire

Jack The Ripper is a vampire, and
Holmes refusal to believe it could lead
to his downfall.

Tales From The Strangers Room

A collection of writings from more
than 20 Sherlockians with author
profits going to The Beacon Society.

The Secret Journal of Dr Watson

Holmes and Watson head to the newly
formed Soviet Union to rescue the
Romanovs.

www.mxpublishing.com